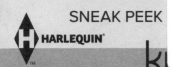

TOO MUCH OF A GOOD THING?

"I'm not looking for anything more than a couple of laughs, some fun."

Lu continued, "I'm not a complete idiot. I know that you're only going to be around for three months and that was just a little bit of getting carried away by the moment. And, frankly, I've just come out of a decade-long relationship with two boys and I gave them every last bit of energy I had. I just want to have some company. I thought maybe you could do with the same."

Company? What was she offering? *Company* company or *sex* company? "Does the company involve getting naked?" he asked in his most prosaic voice.

Judging by the shock that jumped into her eyes, she hadn't reached the bedroom. But then her eyes smoked over and he knew that she wasn't far behind him. Unfortunately along with seeing I-want-to-get-you-naked there was a healthy dose of I-don't-know-what-I'm-doing, as well.

And, anyway, what was *he* thinking? Hadn't he just decided to try something different while he was here in Durban? Yet here he was, sliding right back into old patterns and habit reactions.

"Ah...um...well..." Lu stuttered. *Good God.* "Actually, I had thought about it...."

DEAR READER,

I am so enjoying the Harlequin® KISS™ series, and I wait in eager anticipation (as I'm sure you do, too) to download the new releases every month.

Rugby is a big deal in my part of the world, and we are passionate about our teams—from schoolboy rugby to our national team, the Springboks. I was watching a post-match interview by one of the coaches and I thought, *Mmm-hmm... he's pretty cute.* I love being a romance novelist, so admiring handsome men can be classified as research! *What if he were superhot and a former bad boy of rugby made good...?* And the story started to take shape in my head.

Will comes to Durban on a three-month contract to be the caretaker coach of the city's superstar Stingrays rugby team. Lu, with the twin brothers she raised now at university, is at a loss about what to do now. She wants to revive her flagging career, and by meeting Will she manages to land a job as the Stingrays' press photographer.

They both think that they can ignore the fact that their hair almost catches on fire from the sexual heat they generate... ha-ha-ha!

As per usual, I had the best fun writing this book, and nothing makes me happier than to guide two sexy, headstrong people to their happy-ever-after. Enjoy!

With my very warmest wishes,

Joss xxx

P.S. Come and say hi via Facebook: Joss Wood, Twitter: @josswoodbooks or at Josswoodbooks.wordpress.com

TOO MUCH OF
A GOOD THING?

JOSS WOOD

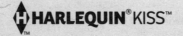

If you purchased this book without a cover you should be aware that this book is stolen property. It was reported as "unsold and destroyed" to the publisher, and neither the author nor the publisher has received any payment for this "stripped book."

Recycling programs
for this product may
not exist in your area.

ISBN-13: 978-0-373-20742-8

TOO MUCH OF A GOOD THING?

Copyright © 2013 by Joss Wood

All rights reserved. Except for use in any review, the reproduction or utilization of this work in whole or in part in any form by any electronic, mechanical or other means, now known or hereafter invented, including xerography, photocopying and recording, or in any information storage or retrieval system, is forbidden without the written permission of the publisher, Harlequin Enterprises Limited, 225 Duncan Mill Road, Don Mills, Ontario, Canada M3B 3K9.

This is a work of fiction. Names, characters, places and incidents are either the product of the author's imagination or are used fictitiously, and any resemblance to actual persons, living or dead, business establishments, events or locales is entirely coincidental.

This edition published by arrangement with Harlequin Books S.A.

For questions and comments about the quality of this book, please contact us at CustomerService@Harlequin.com.

® and TM are trademarks of Harlequin Enterprises Limited or its corporate affiliates. Trademarks indicated with ® are registered in the United States Patent and Trademark Office, the Canadian Trade Marks Office and in other countries.

Printed in U.S.A.

www.Harlequin.com

ABOUT THE AUTHOR

___

Joss Wood wrote her first book at the age of eight and has never really stopped. Her passion for putting letters on a blank screen is matched only by her love of books and travelling—especially to the wild places of Southern Africa—and possibly by her hatred of ironing and making school lunches.

Fueled by coffee, when she's not writing or being a hands-on mum, Joss, with her background in business and marketing, works for a nonprofit organization to promote the local economic development and collective business interests of the area where she resides. Happily and chaotically surrounded by books, family and friends, she lives in KwaZulu-Natal, South Africa, with her husband, children and their many pets.

Other Harlequin® KISS™ titles by Joss Wood:

If You Can't Stand the Heat...
It Was Only a Kiss

This and other titles by Joss Wood are available in ebook format from www.Harlequin.com.

A little over a year ago, on the same day
that I found out that my dream of becoming published
was about to come true, my sister was involved
in the most horrendous car accident.

Because she is the bravest, strongest, most
incredible person I know, this book is dedicated to her.

Love you, Di.

TOO MUCH OF
A GOOD THING?

ONE

—

'Laptop and mobile chargers packed? Did you check the oil in the car?'

Lu Sheppard stood in the east coast early-morning sunshine and, because she knew that throwing her arms around the hairy knees closest to her and hanging on tightly wouldn't be appreciated, jammed her clenched fists into the pockets of her faded denim shorts. Turning her head away, she swallowed furiously before digging deep and yanking out her patented, much practised I'm-OK-you're-OK smile.

'Lu, *you* did,' answered Daniel, the younger of her twin brothers. 'Twice.'

That was right. She had. And she'd ticked it off on the list she'd made for them. Not that either of them had looked at it. Lord, how was she going to *do* this? These boys had been her life and her focus for the past decade. How was she supposed to just let them get into their car and drive across the country to university and, to all intents and purposes, out of her life? She'd yelled at them, cried with them and cried *over* them. She'd provided meals and lifts, helped with homework and bugged them to talk to her. She'd been father, mother, sister and friend.

She was twenty-nine years old and not only was she unable to stare empty nest syndrome in the eye, it was also kicking her non-sexy butt. But, like so many other emotions she'd experienced over the past ten years, the boys didn't have to know that...

Daniel leaned back against the door of his jointly owned car and cleared his throat. Lu saw the look he gave Nate and felt rather than saw the nod Nate gave in reply. Nate moved to stand next to his non-identical twin, equally tall, equally good-looking.

Daniel cleared his throat again. 'Lu, we *are* grateful that you stepped up to be our guardian when Mom and Dad died. If it wasn't for you we would've ended up with some crusty relative who probably would've shipped us off to boarding school and holiday camps.'

Since their parents had both been only children, Daniel's comment wasn't far off the truth. All their relatives were old, crusty, and generally waiting for the light in the tunnel.

'But it's time for a new start...for us and also for you.'

Huh? 'What do you mean?'

Daniel rubbed his jaw. 'We think it's time for you to do all the things you couldn't do because you were raising us.'

Lu frowned. 'Where is this coming from, guys? We talked about this—about you two leaving.'

'Sure—about what uni was like, how we felt about leaving, what we were getting into. But we never spoke about *you*.' Nate chipped in.

Lu's expression was pure confusion. 'Why did we need to? My life isn't changing.'

'It should,' Nate retorted.

'But why?'

'Because nothing about your life is normal for a single woman of your age! When did you last have a date?' Nate demanded.

Lu couldn't remember. It had been a while—six, eight months? She could barely remember the man, just that he hadn't been able to wait to get rid of her after she'd told him that her twin brothers lived with her and she was their guardian. She couldn't blame him; his had been the standard reaction from the very few men she'd dated over the years: shock followed by an immediate desire to find the closest exit.

Add a large house, two dogs, an enormous saltwater fish tank, three corn snakes—no, they'd been moved to a reptile centre when she'd refused to look after them after the boys left—and cats to the pile of her baggage, and it was no wonder her dates belted away.

'We need to talk to you about...*you*,' Nate said.

'Me?' Lu yelped as she pulled a band from her shorts and finger-combed her straight, mouse-brown hair into a stubby pony.

Uh, *no*. She looked after *them*—physically, mentally—they didn't look after her. That was the way their little family worked.

'Look, Lu, we're not only leaving, we're leaving *you*. You know our plans: degrees, then we want to travel. We have no idea where we'll end up but there's a good chance it won't be here,' Nate continued. 'That being said, it would be a lot easier for us if we knew that you were happy and busy and had a full life of your own. Take this house, for instance; we don't want you hanging on to this mansion in the hope that one of us will want it one day. And right now it's a huge house for you to live in by yourself.'

Dan jumped in. 'We're not asking you to sell the house, or anything like that... We just want you to know that we are cool with whatever you want to do with it: sell it, rent it out, start up a commune...'

Lu sat down on the steps leading to the front door and rested her forearms on her thighs. Nate sat down next to her and draped a muscular arm around her shoulder. 'Just please don't become a crazy lady who rattles around here talking to herself and rescuing cats. That was the first thing we wanted to mention...'

There was more? Really? Good grief!

Daniel dropped to his haunches in front of her and pinned her with a look that went far beyond his eighteen years. 'Lu, you are going to be on your own for the first time since you were roughly our age.'

Well, yeah. That was why empty nest syndrome was wiping the floor with her face.

'We want you to have some fun—to live your life.' Daniel raked an agitated hand through his hair, which desperately needed a cut. 'You need to stop being so responsible, to take a breath. To do the things you should've been doing while you were raising us.'

Lu cocked her head. 'Like...?'

'Like clubbing and—' Daniel looked at a point beyond her shoulder and blushed '—hooking up.'

Hooking up? Heavens, if she couldn't remember when last she'd had a date, she'd had absolutely no idea when she last had sex. She suspected she might need a high-pressure cleaner to remove the cobwebs.

'So, here's your "to do" list. We want you to try new things like…skydiving or learning to surf. Pottery classes or dance lessons,' Nate suggested.

Daniel, her brand and fashion-conscious brother, winced at her faded purple T-shirt and battered jeans. 'Some decent clothes would also be a good idea.'

'I *have* decent clothes!' Lu objected.

'Then wear them!' Daniel shot back. 'And your hair needs a cut and you could do with a facial. You need a lifestyle makeover.'

Since their words plucked a chord somewhere deep inside her, she suspected that they might be right. But she certainly didn't have to like it.

Lu growled. 'I hate you.' She glared at Daniel. '*And* you.'

'No, you don't. You love us.'

Nate grinned and her heart flipped over. God, she did. So much. How was she supposed to let them go?

'You *should* go clubbing. Somewhere hip and fun. You'll have to dress up and make an effort.' Nate said. 'Makhosi will take you, Lu.'

Of course he would. Clubbing was her oldest and best friend's favourite way to blow off steam.

'But she has to have a makeover first. I wouldn't be seen with her with that hair!' Daniel added.

'Hey!' Lu protested.

'Haircut, highlights and a makeover,' Daniel stated, and Lu glared at him. 'As Mak has said, more than once, that hair of yours is a disgrace: much better suited to a prissy librarian who doesn't curse, drink wine and who has never had a Big O in her life.'

Well, that sounded like her. Not the wine and the cursing part, but the Big O was definitely true. Could she be so damn emotional because she was sexually frustrated? It would be easy to shift the blame, but the truth was that sex had been scarce—OK, practically non-existent—for most of this past decade, so she couldn't blame her weeping on that.

Empty Nest Syndrome: two. Lu: nil.

And when had her brothers become old enough to mention her orgasms—or lack of them—anyway?

Nate leaned back and put his ankle on his knee. 'But, Lu, more important than anything else...you should get a job.'

Dan shook his head. 'Not that she uses any of it, but there is enough money coming in from the trust. She doesn't have to work if she doesn't want to.'

No, she didn't... If she could bring herself to use the money for anything other than the essentials that kept body and soul together. She had never felt comfortable using her parents' money for anything other than food, shelter and transport.

His brother sent him a you're-a-moron look. 'Not for the money, dude. Because it's something to...to get her teeth into.'

'Oh, right. Good point.'

Lu lifted her fingers and started to tick their demands off. 'So, you two think that if I find a job, go clubbing, have a makeover, learn how to surf—'

'And skydive,' Nate interjected.

'Dream on.' Lu glared at him and continued. 'Go

to pottery and dance lessons then I won't have time to mope?'

Two blond heads nodded to some internal twin beat.

Lu stared past their car down the driveway. The thing was they could be right. The distraction of getting out and about might keep her from going off her head worrying about them. It wasn't a bad idea.

Lu nodded slowly. 'I'll think about it.'

'Promise you'll do it.' Nate insisted.

'I promise to think about it.'

'If you do it, we promise to come home in three months' time,' Nate said slyly.

'You're blackmailing me with a promise to come home?' Lu's mouth dropped open. 'You little snot!'

Nate just grinned and looked at his watch. 'We need to get going, Lu.'

She couldn't bear it. She really couldn't. She struggled to find the words and when she did they were muffled with emotion. 'Call me when you get there. Drive carefully.'

Nate pulled her up, cuddled her, and easily lifted her off her feet before placing a kiss on her cheek. 'Love ya, sis.'

When Nate released her, Daniel held her close. 'Take care of yourself. Have fun. Please, *please* have some fun,' he told her. Daniel let her go and hopped into the passenger seat. 'We'll call you when we get there.'

Lu nodded, touched Daniel's arm resting on the windowsill of the car and blew Nate a kiss.

Her boys...driving off to start their new life...

Lu watched their car turn into the road and sat down on the stairs, holding her face in her hands as she watched her two chicks fly from her very large and now very empty nest.

They would be fine, she assured herself. As for herself...she wasn't quite sure.

Two weeks later, in the VIP area of *Go!* on a very busy Friday night, Will Scott placed his elbows on the railing and looked down at the gyrating masses below him. It was nearly midnight and he'd been thinking about leaving the club for the past half-hour. He could walk down the block to the boutique hotel he'd booked into two days ago and in fifteen minutes could be face-down on the monstrous double bed.

That sounded like heaven.

Will felt someone lean on the railing next to him and looked into the battered face of his best friend Kelby, CEO of the Stingrays rugby franchise, who was also his boss for the next three months. Panic swirled in his gut at the thought.

'How is Carter?' Will asked.

The iconic and surly head coach of the Rays had suffered a heart attack a month back, and as the rugby season was fast approaching the team had been left rudderless without a coach.

'Still in hospital. Still doing tests. They're talking about a bypass,' Kelby replied. 'He said to tell you not to mess it up.'

If it was anyone other than Kelby Will would never utter the words he was about to say.

'The chances are good that I will.' Will rubbed the back of his neck. 'I really don't know if I'm doing the right thing, Kels. This isn't some little local team I'll be caretaker coach of. It's one of the top teams in the premier rugby playing world.'

'It is,' Kelby agreed easily. 'So?'

'So I'm thirty-four years old, not old enough to be a coach, and I have no experience at all! I only retired from international rugby last season and I don't want to muck it up!' Will retorted, shoving his hand into his dark brown hair.

Kelby placed his bottle of beer on a high table and sent him a penetrating look. 'It's strange to see you even marginally unhinged. You are probably the calmest, most confident person I know.'

'I don't feel too confident at the moment,' Will admitted.

'You've been unofficial coach of every team you've ever played for.' Kelby replied, his smile wide. 'I remember that first practice you attended as an eighteen-year-old. You were so full of Kiwi confidence that you told—who was it?—that he was breaking from the scrum too soon.'

Will dropped his head in embarrassment. He'd chirped the then Captain of the England squad and his big mouth had propelled him into a series of initiations by the older players that had quickly taught him to keep his head down and his mouth closed. But Kelby did have a point. Even early in his career he'd had an affinity for telling people what to do.

Rugby was as natural to him as breathing...but coaching? He was a player, not a technician. Kelby kept telling him that he had the assistant coaches for that side of things—a support team who were employed to deal with the technical aspects. His job was to train, to motivate, to strategise, to inspire and to lead. To get results and to win.

But, hey, no pressure.

It was a new ballgame, Will told himself. Something new to conquer. Another challenge to meet. A temporary stop-gap while he decided what he wanted to do for the rest of his life.

Kelby looked contemplative. 'You know, when I offered you this job it was more with hope than expectation. I know you've had other job offers, like commentating, and I also know that your business interests in New Zealand are extensive enough to keep you busy. So why did you accept this job halfway across the world, Will?'

Will shrugged and looked down into the mass of people below. There she was again, her long, lean body dressed in tight jeans and a sparkly emerald-green top. Her elfin face was topped by an ultra-short cap of sun-streaked light brown hair and he wished he could see what colour those light eyes actually were. Blue? Grey? She was talking to the guy she'd spent most of the evening dancing with and he couldn't quite work out the relationship between them. There was a lot of touching, but no kissing, and he frequently left her to dance with different women.

Even at a distance he could see that the guy had charm and he used it...and the woman didn't seem to mind. She just perched on her barstool, politely dismissed the guys trying to pick her up and watched the crowd.

'Will?'

Kelby was still expecting an answer so Will jammed

his hands into the pockets of his jeans and thought about how to answer his question. 'I just wanted to get out of New Zealand for a while...get away from the constant speculation and conversation about why I retired at the peak of my career. About what I'm going to do, whether I'm ever going to settle down.'

'Why *did* you retire at the peak of your career?'

'Exactly that—because it was the peak. Hopefully when people remember my contribution to New Zealand rugby they'll remember the last seven years—not the years I spent before that, trying to flush my career and my life down a toilet.'

'Did you take this job because you felt you owed me?' Kelby demanded. 'Because if you did I'll kick your ass.'

Of course he had. If it hadn't been for Kelby he wouldn't have had a rugby career—wouldn't have captained the team for the past five years, wouldn't be known as one of the best fullbacks in the sport. Three months of his life spent coaching the Rays wouldn't even come close to paying his debt.

'I do owe you.'

Kelby shook his head. 'You just had your head too far up your own backside and I yanked it out.'

Will shook his head. Only Kelby could describe his self-destructive behaviour so lightly.

'You repaid your debt to me by straightening out your life. But, like with everything else, you, being you, have to take everything to the nth degree,' Kelby added, resting his elbows on the railing that overlooked the heaving club below.

Will's grin faded at Kelby's serious face. 'What are you talking about?'

'Both you and Jo became too successful, too young... and it went to your heads. Jo was the bad girl of professional sports, and because you wanted to get into and stay in her pants she pulled you into her crazy lifestyle.'

'Sex, drugs and rock and roll,' Will said bitterly. 'Then I married her.'

'And, because you're a competitive SOB you thought that whatever she could do you could do better. God, the press loved you two.'

Thanks to their exploits, they'd sold so many newspapers that the holding companies should have offered them shares, Will thought sourly. They'd fallen into bed within an hour of meeting each other, been married within a month. Theirs had been an instant sexual connection, an adrenaline-filled lust that had been as compelling as it was dangerous.

'Jo did walk on the wild side and I loved it. The clubbing, the drinking, dallying with recreational drugs.'

Then had come the hell of trying to juggle their schedules to be together, the massive fights when they did meet up, and his slowly dawning realisation that they didn't have anything keeping them together other than a waning sexual chemistry.

'But what's that got to do with being competitive?'

'After the divorce you wanted to show Jo that you didn't need her to have a good time. The parties got bigger, there were different girls every night, and you were still making the papers for all the wrong reasons.'

'Nearly losing my career by pitching up at practice either drunk or constantly hungover. Yes, I remember! You covered for me that entire season. When the management team threatened to fire me you promised them that you could straighten me out, why?'

'You were too talented to be allowed to mess up your life,' Kelby stated.

Will shuddered. If Kelby hadn't stepped up and fought for him to stay employed by the rugby franchise there would've been no captaincy, no career.

Damn straight he owed him.

'But I didn't think I'd create a Frankenstein! When you finally heard my come-to-the-light talk you went from Mr Wild to Mr Disciplined Control. You hardly drink, you're rabidly anti-drugs, and you never allow yourself to have a relationship that lasts longer than a night. Maybe two.'

'The spark usually only lasts that long,' Will muttered. Bitter experience and a couple of brief affairs had taught him that the hotter the sexual flare of attraction, the quicker the flame died.

'Fires need to be fed, Will. Your problem is that you think sex fuels a relationship. It doesn't. Not long-term anyway. Love fuels sex. Maybe if you tried getting to know a woman first before taking her to bed you would actually learn this.' Kelby sent him a knowing look. 'Or maybe you *do* know this and that's why you limit yourself to one-or two-night stands. You don't allow yourself to get to know anyone because you don't want to risk falling in love.'

Why would he want to fall in love? Love was the pits! A rollercoaster ride of hot sex, huge fights and total loss of control. Control...he *never* lost it. Not any more. Not on the field, not in relationships, never in the bedroom. It reminded him of who he'd been and he didn't like it. Didn't want to be reminded of it.

'Have you been taking some of Angie's girl pills?' Will demanded. 'Geez, you sound like one of my sisters!'

Yet Kelby wouldn't shut up. 'Here's an idea...why don't you try being friends with a woman instead?'

'That's not the way it works.'

'On planet Normal it does,' Kelby retorted.

Will couldn't find a clever retort so he fell back on an old, trusted response. 'Shuddup.'

Kelby just snorted into his beer.

Will looked over the railing to see some of his team in the heaving mass of dancers below, surrounded by a lot of nubile, barely dressed female flesh. They were so young and so obvious. He looked right, to the woman at the bar who was the complete opposite of them. Older, but inadvertently sexy, he mused, fascinated by her. Understated, yet compelling, with her minimal make-up and short, no-fuss hair.

Kelby banged his empty bottle down on the table. 'Let's get out of here.'

Will nodded and drained his beer. His eyes swept over the crowd below and he saw that she was still there, standing by the bar, a long glass of what looked like mineral water in her hand. Unlike the rest of the clubbers she looked completely sober, and when she lifted her arm, and swung her watch-bracelet around her arm, he saw that she was checking the time. Her body language screamed that she wanted to leave and he was momentarily disappointed not to have met her.

You're here for three months only. Sex was important

to him, although he was still weary of casual hookups. But as the thought of a permanent relationship gave him hives it didn't leave him with a lot of options. What could be worse than being trapped in a relationship with someone after familiarity and boredom had snuffed out all sexual attraction? It had happened with Jo, consistently rated as one of the world's sexiest sportswomen, so it was bound to happen with anyone else.

If he got bored, fell out of lust and couldn't maintain a relationship with someone as hot as *her*, he held out little—actually, *no* hope that he could do it with someone more...normal. He was, he admitted, a dysfunctional ass when it came to women.

As Will and Kelby walked down the steps from the VIP area he debated which exit to use. If he turned right it would take him past the bar and he might see the woman again.

Not that he'd do anything about it when he saw her; he just wanted to satisfy his curiosity about the colour of her eyes.

He traded high-fives with the more sober clubbers and rugby fans who recognised him, and Kelby willingly allowed himself to be pulled into a conversation with a couple of devoted fans. Rugby talk and free beer. Will grinned. Kelby couldn't resist either.

Will dismissed the raucous comments flung his way and flatly ignored the offers from women—and one camp man—to buy him a drink. It took him about fifteen minutes to get to where he'd last seen her and he looked around. She'd disappeared.

Gone.

Later, he couldn't have said why he looked in that direction, what made him glance over his shoulder. But there she was again. Except this time she was swaying on her feet. A large man, one whom he hadn't seen before, had put his arm around her shoulder and pulled her into his side. She wasn't resisting. She just looked past him with glassy eyes and her head bobbed on her neck.

She was high as a friggin' satellite.

Will frowned. Fifteen minutes ago she'd been dead sober and wanting to go home—now she was spaced.

He knew drugs—could spot the signs—but he was convinced she'd been telling her friend that she wanted to go home. Why take a hit if she wanted to leave? And whatever she'd taken had propelled her into la-la land very, very quickly.

Will looked at her and his gut instinct screamed that something was wrong. He really didn't like the look of the broad, hairy hand that was cupping her ribcage, one grubby-looking thumb resting just under the curve of her breast. She'd refused the advances of far better-looking and better-dressed men than him the whole evening. There was no way that she'd hook up with that jackass now.

Date-rape drug. The thought slammed into his head with the force of a rugby scrum.

And where the hell was her friend...boyfriend... date—whatever he was? Will gnawed his bottom lip and swore, considering what to do. He was ninety-nine percent sure that her drink had been spiked, and if it had been, he couldn't just leave her. Who knew what would happen to her?

But...what if he was wrong? This could all be con-sensual and he could be grabbing the wrong end of a very sharp stick. But it would be far, far worse for her if he was right and he left her on her own.

Oh, well, here goes nothing, he thought as he ap-proached them, pulling a name out of the air. 'Flora? Hey—*hi!* I never expected to bump into you here!'

TWO

—

Disconnected memories and snippets of conversation jumped in and out of her brain as Lu struggled to open her eyes. Eventually she just kept them closed and let herself drift. She remembered a friendly argument with Mak about her new, super-short hair. She didn't think it suited her, and she thought her newly plucked eyebrows were shaped in too thin a line. Mak had snorted that she had the fashion sense of a goat and that she looked fabulous. Rolling backwards in her memories, she saw Mak arriving at her house with skinny jeans, too expensive shoes and a sparkly top, because the boys had been gone two weeks already and he was tired of her moping so he was taking her clubbing.

When was that...? Today? Yesterday?

No, last night she'd been at that club, watching Mak's broad back slink off to the dance floor for one more dance while she waited for him at the bar.

Then...nothing.

Lu forced her eyes open, blinked and rubbed her

eyes. When she opened them again they focused on a handsome face lying on the pillow next to her. Her eyes drifted over his long frame, over his muscled arm down to the tanned, broad hand that rested lightly on the top of her much whiter thigh. A masculine hand with a light touch... It felt so right, she thought as her eyelids drooped closed again.

OK, this dream was too awesome to lose by waking up.

Lu had no idea how much time passed before she woke again, but in contrast to the last time this time she didn't feel as if she had cotton candy clouds stuffed in her head. There wouldn't be a man lying next to her.

Lu opened one eye and—*holy mackerel!*—there still was a man. In bed.

With her?

And not just any man. A tall, dark and sexy one, who ticked all her make-me-hum boxes. Broad shoulders—tick. Muscular arms and chest—tick, tick. Long, powerful legs and slim hips. A face that was utterly masculine, a strong jaw and a battered nose that kept him from being over-the-top gorgeous.

Tick, tick, tick, tick, tick...

When he opened his eyes would they be an intense blue or green? They were neither. Just amber...the rich, deep hue of expensive sherry...edged with stubby dark lashes. They blinked once, twice, and then he yawned and she could see excellent teeth and...tonsils.

Tonsils? Seriously?

'Oh, crap!' he said as he rolled off the bed to his feet. He held out his hands as Lu scooted up the bed and wrapped her arms around her knees. 'Don't freak!'

Strangely, she wasn't close to panicking, but he looked as if he was about to.

'How do you feel?' he demanded. 'Are you OK?'

Was she? Lu considered his question. She was in a strange, albeit expensive hotel room, with a man who dinged her personal hotness bell, and she had no idea who he was or how she'd got there.

There was only one logical explanation for waking up in a strange man's bed. *What* was it that she'd tossed down her throat—and how much?—that she couldn't remember having sex with such an attractive man? It had to be the equivalent of an alcoholic bravery pill, because she *never* did casual hook-ups.

Lord, she prayed that he used a condom.

Right—there was only one way to get through this, she thought. *Keep calm. Play it cool. Act your socks off.* After raising two boys she was a master at putting on a 'happy face' to get through any awkward or emotional situation.

She put on a fake smile and met his brilliant eyes. 'So, that was fun. Thanks. I'll just get dressed and get out of your hair.'

Lu forced the words out and held her breath when he placed his hands on hips covered in black low-slung boxers. He topped six feet by a couple of inches and, because the navy T-shirt and boxers left little to the imagination, he radiated physical power. *Why* did he seem so familiar?

Heavy brows lifted before dropping into a frown. 'Fun?'

Oh, good Lord! Hadn't he enjoyed it? Was she *that* out of practice? Lu felt heat creep up her neck and into

her cheeks. 'I'm sorry, I'm not very experienced at...'
she waved her hand at the crumpled sheets '...this.
Look, let me just get out of here and we can both pretend it didn't happen.'

Laughter flashed in his eyes and the corners of his
mouth twitched. Lu felt the heat on her cheeks inten-
sify. 'What do you think happened last night?'

Lu stared at her bare knees. 'I'm presuming that
we had bad sex.'

'You don't remember?'

'Hence the word *presuming*,' Lu snapped. 'Did we
sleep together?'

'Uh, not in the biblical sense.' He crossed his arms
across his chest and those spectacular biceps bulged.
His mouth flirted with a smile. 'And, for the record,
men don't *ever* have bad sex. There's OK sex, blow-
your-head-off hot sex and everything in between. But
bad sex? Not so much.'

'Thanks for the update,' Lu muttered. 'So, nothing
happened?'

'No, nothing happened...sex-wise.'

Damn, was that disappointment she felt? OK, even
if she couldn't remember it, re-losing her virginity—
and after so long she was pretty sure that she could be
reclassified—to such a wonderful-looking man could
only have been a fabulous thing.

A headache she hadn't been aware of started pulsing behind her eyes as confusion swirled around her
head. 'So, if I didn't sleep with you then why am I half
undressed and in your bed? Bra less? Did I say I would
and then pass out? Should I start feeling scared?' But

she didn't. Not yet. Weird, yes. Confused, definitely. Scared? Not so much.

'I promise that you are safe.' He must have sensed her confusion.

Lu looked into his sincere eyes and nodded. She wasn't sure why but her gut was saying that she could trust him—that despite his size he wouldn't lay a finger on her.

He sat down in the chair to one side of the bed and rested his forearms on his knees. After a short silence he spoke again. 'I'm Will Scott, by the way.'

Will Scott! She'd thought he looked familiar. What on earth was she doing in the hotel room of the new—crackling hot—coach of Durban's super-starry rugby team?

'Ah...'

'Do you want coffee? I need coffee. Actually, I need a drink. But coffee will have to do.' Will stood up and walked over to the phone next to the bed, placed the order with Room Service.

Lu pulled up the neck of the T-shirt that had fallen halfway down her shoulder. His shirt, obviously. Which meant...what? Had he undressed her? And if they hadn't slept together why was she out of her clothes?

'Where are my clothes?' she asked, unable to forget that she wasn't wearing a bra.

'Bathroom. Disgusting,' Will replied. 'You vomited all over yourself.'

Lu winced. OK, gross. Gross to the factor of four hundred. This story just kept getting better...*not!*

'Why did I vomit? I never drink enough to vomit. I don't understand.'

Lu dropped her legs and swung them off the side of the bed. For a moment she thought she saw Will's eyes on them, but when she looked at him again he was staring at the beige carpet beneath his bare feet.

'What happened to me?' Lu questioned as she stood up and his shirt fell to just above her knees. Of course it still revealed most of her shoulder, but better that than her naked breasts...though she suspected he'd already seen those since he'd undressed her.

'I saw you in the club and you looked sober. The next time I saw you—*Lu*—you looked spaced...high. You were also in the arms of a man I hadn't seen you with and he agreed that your name was Flora.'

'Flora? Who is Flora?' Lu demanded. 'And if we've never met before how do you know my name?'

'Oh, you have some business cards in your wallet. After I got you settled I went through it to try and find someone I could contact for you.'

That made sense. She did have business cards in her wallet that she occasionally handed out to promote her photography.

'So, you saw me with this guy...?' Lu prompted.

'I pulled the name Flora out of the air and he went along with it. That was a pretty big clue that something wasn't right. So I grabbed hold of you and tried to figure out a way to attract a bouncer's attention. Then you puked all over him. And yourself. And my shoes,' Will added ruefully.

Lu closed her eyes. 'Oh...hell. Seriously?'

Will nodded. 'Thank God you did. Puking probably

saved your life. You got all the rest of that undigested date-rape drug out of your system.'

Lu blinked and held up her hand. '*Whoa!* Date-rape drug? What date rape drug? *What?*'

'It's the only reason why a stone-cold sober person would be reduced to a high, spaced-out, unresponsive robot in fifteen minutes,' Will explained.

Lu felt the pounding in her head increase, followed by an unpleasant whirling sensation. Date-rape drug? Lu staggered to the edge of the bed, dropped down and felt nausea building in her throat. She could have been held hostage, raped repeatedly, subjected to indescribably disgusting acts...

In her head she was screaming, panic was bubbling, and she bit down hard on her bottom lip to keep from whimpering. She would not cry. She would not lose control, she thought as stark images conjured up by her imagination—hard and cruel—slapped her again and again.

She couldn't get any air...she needed air.

Will crouched in front of her, his arm resting on his knee. 'That's quite an impressive show of control. Most girls would be hysterical by now. Right—now, breathe. The important point is to remember that nothing happened. I took you away after you threw up. So just breathe, slow and deep.' It was the voice from her dreams, calm, steady. In control. The images disappeared.

'But...'

'Nothing happened, Lu.'

Will hooked her chin and made her look into his calm face. She could see hot rage bubbling in his eyes...

for her? She grabbed his wrist and held onto to him, needing his steadiness, needing the contact, needing to lean, just for a minute, on his strength.

She sucked in more air. 'OK, nothing happened. You're sure?'

'Very sure. A thousand percent sure. You were in my sight the entire time, apart from the fifteen minutes just after your drink was spiked. You've only been alone with me the entire time. Believe me?'

She did.

'Your mobile is dead, so I couldn't contact anyone, but I took you to the closest hospital, they pumped your stomach and you stayed there the night.'

'*What?* I stayed the night in hospital?'

Will nodded, his face grim.

'So today isn't today, it's tomorrow?' Lu cried. 'I lost an entire day?'

Will grimaced. 'Yeah. You came round for a while this afternoon and the doctors thought that you were well enough to be discharged, provided someone kept an eye on you.'

'I don't remember anything!'

'Apparently that's normal.'

'That's your opinion. Nothing is vaguely normal about this. So you brought me back here?' Lu looked around. 'Where *is* here?'

'The Bay—penthouse suite. My temporary quarters until I find a flat to rent. Well, I didn't know who to contact, and I couldn't leave you alone, so I changed you into one of my T-shirts and let you sleep it off.'

Lu looked at the bed they'd shared. 'You slept with me?'

'Just to keep an eye on you,' Will reassured her. 'You were having some nasty dreams. Judging by your quick downhill slide, the hospital doctors think it was GHB, which is very easy to overdose on. You were very lucky. Because you weigh next to nothing, the doctors were worried. An overdose can lead to a coma or death. '

'I never leave my drink unattended,' Lu protested.

'You did. You put it on the bar when your friend came back from the dance floor. You checked the time...' Will cursed.

Lu raised her eyebrows. He'd been watching her? How? From where? And yet she still didn't feel creeped out. Just protected...and safe. As if she had a burly guardian angel looking after her.

Will closed his eyes for a millisecond. 'You were directly below me. I was watching the action from the VIP area above.

'Now I sound like a stalker.' He raked his hand through his short hair and grimaced. 'I'm not, I promise. I saw you. You looked sober. The next time I saw you, you looked high, with someone I hadn't seen you even speak to. Something just didn't seem right.'

Lu believed him. Maybe she was being naïve or dumb, but she knew, to the bottom of her toes, that Will had saved her. Besides, seriously, why would anyone who looked like him need a date-rape drug to get a girl into bed? He was probably beating them off with clubs as it was.

She wasn't a celeb-watcher but his profile was high enough that it was hard *not* to read about him. He was the ex-bad-boy of international rugby who dated supermodels and superstars. His ex-wife was the Golden

Princess of women's professional tennis, with a face and body that could launch intergalactic starships. And he was an international rugby god—one of New Zealand's national treasures, Lu thought as she remembered the twins' many conversations about him. He was a multi-capped player and had been instrumental in leading his team to victory in the last World Cup. He'd just retired from international rugby and was in Durban for a few months.

Lu was snapped back to the present by a sharp rap on the suite door. Will smiled and her stomach rolled. *Hoo-boy!* Mega-attractive man.

'Coffee. It's about time.' Will moved to the door and looked at her over his shoulder. 'My mobile is next to the bed, or use the hotel phone to contact anyone you need to.'

'Thank you. I will...after I use the bathroom. And Will?'

Lu swallowed and lifted her hands when he turned and looked at her.

'Thank you. It sounds inadequate, but I am so, so grateful. For everything. I am forever in your debt.'

Lu washed up and held each side of the free-standing basin, staring down into the expanse of white porcelain. Why did she feel nineteen again? Defenceless, vulnerable, scared... It had to be because, like before, she'd been dumped into this horrible situation without any warning, any time to prepare.

It was a situation she couldn't control and she was propelled back to that black time when she'd felt sick with grief, crippled by the responsibility of her new role as guardian to her brothers, feeling so helpless.

Every insecurity she'd ever had came rushing back—every sadness, every fear. Oh, she knew intellectually that this wasn't her fault, but knowing was different from feeling, and being at the mercy of whoever it was who'd spiked her drink scared her down to her toes. Added to that was the realisation that she'd been in Will's hands, his care...under his power.

She wanted to curl up in a corner and suck her thumb. GHB? Spiked drinks? A high-profile celebrity rescuing her from what might have been a very nasty situation? Incidents like this didn't happen to ordinary girls like her. If she thought about what could have happened...

Lu bumped her hand against her forehead in an effort to clear the cobwebs and realised that her stomach was rebelling again.

Don't think about it. Don't think about it...

Will's face popped into her head and she focused on that as a distraction. He was so much better-looking in real life than in the newspapers and on TV. They didn't capture the intelligence in those topaz-coloured eyes, the flicker of movement in that mobile mouth, the very, very small dimple-type dent that appeared in his cheek when he smiled.

And she wasn't even going to *think* about his body... fit, hard, utterly—shockingly!—masculine. Lu rubbed her thighs together. Strangely, she suddenly felt a pounding pulse in a place where she'd never pulsed before.

Lu raised her head to look at herself in the mirror

above the sink and yelped at her reflection. Her brand-new, streaky gold hair that had looked so fabulously chic last night now stood up in tufts on the right side of her head and lay dead flat on the other side. She was sheet-white, her freckles the only bit of colour in her face, and someone had painted the bags under her eyes a bright purple.

No wonder Will Scott had belted out of bed as if the hounds of hell were snapping at his heels. Admittedly her eyes were an unusual colour—sometimes green, sometimes blue—but the spray of freckles across her nose and cheeks were the bane of her life. She was more 'girl next door' than 'I am woman, hear me roar'.

This morning she barely reached 'I am human, hear me whimper'.

So any ideas that he'd been looking at her legs or mouth or any quick flashes of interest she'd thought she'd caught in his eyes was just a very optimistic dose of wishful thinking. *Stupid girl.* Lu pulled a tongue at her reflection, opened the tap and splashed warm water on her face. Stealing a bit of Will's toothpaste, she brushed her teeth with her finger and helped herself to a healthy swig of his mouthwash.

She wet her hands and ran them through her hair in an attempt to look less like a neurotic bantam chicken. She wished she could pull on her clothes, but when she reached for the packet containing them one whiff of the contents had her changing her mind. Will's T-shirt, which barely hit her knees would have to do for now.

Right—she felt marginally human and slightly better able to deal with Will, his smack-you-in-the-face sex appeal and this very weird situation. Lu straightened her spine and opened the bathroom door just as Will walked across from the closet, now dressed in hip hugging faded Levi's, a fire-engine-red T-shirt clutched loosely in his hand.

His chest was lightly covered in dark hair and he had a six-pack that would make a male model jealous. It made her mouth water.

I am woman, see me drool.

'Lu! Lu, where the hell are you?'

Forty-five minutes later a pounding on the suite door and an upset male voice caused Lu to jump in her chair. Will lifted his eyebrows as Lu went to answer the door and the handsome guy from the club pulled her into his arms and whirled her around.

'Bloody hell, Lu. I take you clubbing one frickin' time and you disappear on me! And what the hell were you saying about your drink being spiked? And keep your damned mobile charged, woman!' he bellowed.

Not allowing her to reply, he segued into a barrage of Zulu. While Will didn't understand one individual word, he got the gist. It was the universal tone of you-scared-the-crap-out-of-me.

Lu interrupted him by placing her hand over his mouth. 'Mak Sibaya—Will Scott.'

Mak pushed her hand away, lifted his own hand in a half-greeting and carried on ranting. 'I left you for one dance...I came back and you were gone! I thought you'd done your normal I'm-sick-of-waiting trick and left on your own. When I couldn't get hold of you by yesterday afternoon I went around to the house. When I saw your car was there but you weren't I started to freak.

I'm *still* freaking! And what were you saying about a date-rape drug? What the—'

'She's fine,' Will stated, shoving a cup of coffee into Mak's hand and cutting off another barrage of colourful swear words. 'Did you bring clothes?'

Mak sat down and looked around, eventually pointing to the plastic bag he'd dropped by the door. Will stood up and went to retrieve it, understanding that Mak needed a minute to compose himself—that he'd been seriously worried and expressed it by acting like a jerk. He couldn't blame the guy. It was what guys did when they were unhappy. Any man would be jumping the walls if his woman vanished on him and he couldn't get hold of her.

There was another reason not to have a partner or a girlfriend...you couldn't get agitated and upset if there was no one to get agitated and upset about. And he still wasn't impressed that Mak hadn't taken better care of her at the club—kept his eye on Lu instead of leaving her alone at the bar.

Will sat in the chair opposite Mak and poured himself a cup of coffee. They waited in an uneasy silence as Lu dressed in the next room.

Mak lifted his head and his dark eyes looked miserable when they connected with Will's. 'Thanks, by the way. If anything had happened to her...'

Uncomfortable with the level of emotion he heard in the other man's voice, Will shifted in his seat. 'Sure...I'm glad I was there.'

'Me too.' Mak scrubbed his face with his hands. 'Lu is...she's—'

His words were cut off by Lu's return. Will's T-shirt

had been replaced by a snug, cropped T-shirt of pale pink, revealing an inch of her belly above the band of low-cut white shorts. Long legs ended in a pair of battered flip-flops. She crossed them as she sat down on the couch next to him.

Will handed her a cup of coffee. 'Black. Add what you want to it.' He gestured to the milk and sugar on the tray. Lu, he noticed, took hers black and sweet.

'I hope we're not keeping you from anything?' Lu said after sipping and sighing.

'I have some press interviews scheduled for later, but I'm not in any rush.' Will placed his cup on the tray and leaned forward. 'What do you want to do about the other night? Do you want to press charges?' He watched Lu think.

'I don't know. I feel fine now. A bit of a headache, but that's it.' She dropped her elbows to her knees and rested her face in her hands. 'I'd go to the police but I don't remember a damn thing.'

Will's voice hardened. 'I do. I can give the police an idea of who we're looking for.'

'Except that we can't prove the man you saw me with spiked my drink. He could say that he was helping me,' Lu pointed out.

Will felt his back teeth grind together as the truth of her words registered. 'True, but I still think you should report it.'

Lu placed her thumbnail between her front teeth. 'You're right. It's irresponsible not to.'

'I'll take you, Lu,' said Mak as he placed his empty cup on the coffee table.

He looked calmer, Will thought, less wild-eyed.

Lu angled her head so that she could look at the face of Mak's watch. 'Today *is* Monday, right?'

Mak nodded.

'You can't take me anywhere. You have thirty minutes to get to that preliminary interview at the school. That's all the way across town. '

It took a moment for her words to register, but when they did Mak shot out of his chair and looked panicked. 'I don't want Deon going to that school.'

'It's a back-up plan, Makhosi. We discussed this. It's just in case he doesn't get into St Clare's.'

'You're right—I know you are right. But I don't have time to take you home, get him, and get across town in time for the interview. Is there any chance you can hang on here until I can get back?' Mak asked.

'Lu and I will go to the police and then I can run her home,' Will suggested.

Mak threw him a relieved smile. 'Thanks, Will. I appreciate it.'

Will stood up to shake Mak's hand. He clenched his jaw as he watched Mak and Lu exchange another tender embrace and then Mak was flying out of the door.

Lu shut the door behind him and shook her head. 'Mak only operates at warp speed.' She flicked her thumbnail against her teeth as she walked back towards him. 'You've already done so much. I couldn't impose on you any more. I'll be fine on my own. I'll go to the police and then I'll find my way home.'

Will resisted the impulse to grab her hand and to tell her to relax, to calm down. 'We'll go together,' he insisted and saw her shoulders drop from around her ears. She'd be fine on her own, his ass. But why did he care?

The girl had had her drink spiked, he reminded himself. If he hadn't interfered she could've been raped, subjected to abuse... Will ground his teeth as his blood pressure spiked. Damn straight he'd go to the police with her.

'Maybe I should just write it off as a bad experience and avoid clubs—no matter what my brothers want me to do,' Lu said, picking up her cup again.

'What do your brothers have to do with you clubbing?' Will asked, intrigued.

'Ah...they think I need to get out more,' Lu explained.

He felt disappointed when she waved her words away.

'It's a long story which you'd probably find boring.'

Strangely, he thought he wouldn't. Sure, she wasn't glamorous or glossy, like the women he normally came into contact with, but he had a feeling that Lu was far more interesting than most of the women he met. There was something settled about her...calm, down to earth...*wise*.

He admired her coolness under pressure. Her assumption that they'd slept together had been funny because she'd had a good excuse to lose it earlier. Instead she'd reined in her emotions and thought the situation through, keeping calm and in control, her emotions in check. He'd been dreading having to deal with a weepy, scared creature and her undramatic reaction had been a very welcome relief.

Impressive. He valued keeping his control and he admired her ability to do the same.

And those eyes, God...a mermaid's eyes, reflecting the greens and blues and aquas of a tropical sea.

Will rested his head against the back of the wingback chair and thought that his brief visit to Durban had started off on a very interesting note.

THREE

—

Will turned into the driveway Lu indicated and parked in front of the huge iron gate as she scrabbled in her bag for her keys. He looked through the bars of the gate to the huge, sprawling house with its deep, wraparound veranda and nodded his approval. With a haphazard garden and pitched roof, it looked as a house should—homely and lived in. Big.

Will looked through the gap between the house and the garage and caught a glimpse of the sea. 'This is home?'

'Yep,' Lu said. 'Thanks for the lift and for coming to the police station with me. You were a lot calmer than Mak would've been.'

'He probably would've shouted at you the whole time,' Will stated calmly.

'He did go a bit berserk, didn't he? Sorry about that.'

Will's fingers tightened around the steering wheel. 'He's crazy about you. How long have you been together?'

Lu sent him a puzzled look. 'We're not. Why would you think that?'

Oh, maybe the fact that he kissed you on your mouth, whirled you around and wouldn't stop touching you! Freaking big clues!

'My mistake,' Will said aloud, but he wasn't convinced. And that wasn't jealousy he felt. It couldn't be. He didn't know what it was, but it wasn't jealousy.

'He used to live next door to us and we remained friends when he moved. Mak is just...intense. Protective of me. He adores me, but we're only friends,' Lu explained as the gate slid open.

Yeah, and rugby isn't a contact sport, Will thought as he drove up the circular driveway to her front door. She might think they were only friends, but he was a man and he knew how men acted and thought. How could Mak *not* want to sleep with her? She was gorgeous! A natural beauty with those incredible eyes...

'I saw the look on your face...you think that Mak was irresponsible because he lost track of me.'

He couldn't deny it.

Lu sighed. 'He isn't—not really. He just has a lot on his plate, and when he gets time to step away, to socialise, he goes at it full tilt. And I'm not the type of girl that needs to be looked after...Mak knew that I wanted to go home and I knew that he wanted to stay. I've left him behind at many functions, so he wouldn't have thought it unusual. I have taxi companies on speed dial.'

Will just lifted his eyebrows and looked unconvinced.

His mobile rang. He pressed a button on the steering wheel to activate the hands free and greeted his caller. Lu felt that she should give him some privacy to take his call and tried to get out of the car, but his hand on her arm kept her firmly in place.

Through the car speakers somebody whose name she didn't catch was talking about that afternoon's press conference and Lu listened as Will was briefed on the questions he could expect.

'And obviously there will be the usual questions about your ex-wife.'

'Yeah, OK, I'm *so* happy to answer those!' Will barked, obviously frustrated.

She didn't need a degree in sarcasm to realise that he really *didn't* want to answer any questions on his old life, ex-wife and their marriage.

'Jo's blonde, gorgeous and successful. You're handsome, talented and successful. She's still single. So are you. You were once married and everyone still wants to know what happened to your marriage,' the voice replied calmly. 'The press know there's a story there and they want it.'

'They can all get...' Will shot Lu a look and swallowed the word he wanted to use. 'Stuffed. As per normal, Jo and anything to do with her is off the table, not open for discussion. It was all so long ago you'd think they'd get over it.'

With Will's hand still holding her arm, Lu stayed where she was and thought that they couldn't be more different if they tried. Like Mak, like her parents, even her brothers, Will was a breed apart. One of those successful, innately confident, very-sure-of-their-niche-in-the-world people.

She wanted to be like that.

She didn't have a niche. Her place—her space—had been ripped away when her parents died, and two weeks ago when her brothers had left it had shifted again.

After a decade of the twins being the centre of her world she was alone, and she had to live in this empty house without the daily responsibility of being their guardian. No more suppers to cook, errands to run, parties to keep an eye on. For the first time in her life she wasn't defined by her relationship to her popular parents and her orphaned twin brothers.

Isolation and loneliness kept creeping closer, and she frequently felt ill-equipped to cope with a life that didn't have the twins in it. If she wasn't careful she could slide over the edge into self-pity, and from there it was a slippery slope to depression. She couldn't—refused—to let that happen.

She had to do something about her life, and quickly. After everything that life had thrown at her so far she refused to buckle under because she was alone and feeling at sea. That was why she'd agreed to go clubbing with Mak. She'd realised that she had to get out of the house, out of her own head. The boys were right. She had to start living her life.

Of course getting her drink spiked was an embarrassing start.

It had been a tough decade, she admitted as Will lifted his hand from her arm and carried on with his conversation. She had just started exploring her options for a career when she'd been catapulted without warning into caring for the twins. With the inheritance covering her basic costs she'd run around her brothers, caught up in making their world as secure as she possibility could, determined that they wouldn't feel as lost, as alone and as scared as she did. She'd kept herself and them active and busy in order to keep the grief at bay, and while she'd tried to keep up with her photography she hadn't been able to give it the dedication it required for her to succeed. Somewhere along the way she'd stopped thinking about herself, her place in the world and what excited her.

Who *was* she? Lu was terrified to realise that she hadn't the slightest clue. It was OK, she told herself. She had time to figure it all out. She just needed a plan.

'Sorry about that.' Will's voice pulled her back to the present. 'Lu? Are you OK?'

Lu blinked and focused on his face. Will, so very up close and personal, was even more mouth-wateringly, panty-crumpling, breath-hitchingly gorgeous than any photo anywhere. He wasn't perfect—that would be far too intimidating—and she liked his flaws as much as she liked the rest of the package. Creases at the corner of those warm eyes, and his deep brown hair was, sadly, six inches too short. He had stubby eyelashes and untamed brows and a slash of a nose.

'Do you want me to come in with you? Are you going to be OK?' Will asked.

'I've taken far too much of your time already,' Lu replied, glad to hear that her voice was reasonably steady. 'Thank you for all your help. As I said, I am in your debt.'

Will's eyes tracked over her face. 'If you start re-membering anything and you have questions you're welcome to give me a call at the rugby union. They'll make sure that I get the message and I'll get back to you.'

It was a nice offer, Lu thought, noticing that he didn't give her his mobile number. She wasn't that out of practice that she didn't recognise the gentle brush-off . He wouldn't call again and she could live with that.

After all, she had her own life to get back on track. She didn't need the distraction of a super-sexy rugby player.

But, damn, how she wished they *had* had sex. Just one little time and preferably of the blow-your-head-off variety. Just to...you know...clean those cobwebs out...

Two days later Lu sat on the floor between her leather couch and her coffee table, her laptop in front of her. She was updating her website in an effort to attract more photography work and thought she'd made pretty good progress. The site was hipper and brighter than before, and she liked the photos she'd put on the front page. There was the Johnsons' newborn baby, stark naked with a bright blue bow tied around his tummy and a tag that read 'Special Delivery'. Below that was her favourite photograph of a bridal couple, caught in a loving look so profound it made her throat catch every time she looked at it.

She was good at it, she mused. Capable of capturing the essence of the moment. And now that she had the time to devote to it she realised how much she missed being behind a camera. She'd tried to establish herself as a photographer a couple of times over the past decade, but every opportunity had fizzled out. She'd been offered an apprenticeship under one of the better photographers in the city about a year after her parents had died, but when she'd realised that after-hours work and out-of-town shoots were a standard condition of her employment she'd resigned because she had to be at home for the twins.

She'd done small weddings, worked part-time in a photographic studio before it had closed down six months ago, and done some freelance graphic work, but she hadn't, because of her family situation, been able to land her big break. Her fellow students from photography school were flying and she was ten years behind.

It wouldn't take much to kick-start her business. She had a studio already outfitted in the cottage next to the main house: lights, props and backgrounds. She just needed the clients to get back on track; she *had* to make up for all this lost time.

Her mobile buzzed on the floor next to her and she frowned at the unfamiliar number. Debating whether to answer it, she took a sip of wine and wondered whether she felt like speaking to anyone. *You're becoming a hermit,* she chided herself as she pushed the green button. *Six steps away from becoming that self-conversing, crazy cat lady the twins mentioned.*

'Lu? It's Will Scott.'

Lu's eyebrows shot up as her mouth dried up. Of all the people she'd expected to be on the other end of the call Will was last on her list.

'Um...hi...'

'I called to see how you were doing? Whether you had any lasting effects from the drug?'

'No, I'm fine.'

'Nightmares?' Will demanded.

'One or two,' Lu admitted. 'Normally when I let myself think about what could've happened. Uh...how did you get my number?'

Lu swore that she heard his lips pull up into that super-sexy grin. 'I swiped one of your business cards from your wallet. I see that you freelance...how's the photography business?'

'Slow, actually. I was just updating my site and racking my brain about how to get more clients. How's the rugby coaching business?'

Will's sigh was a combination of frustration and weariness. 'Honestly? Right now it's a pain in my ass. I have some squad members who have the maturity of a two-year-old.'

Lu leaned back against the couch and took a sip from her glass of wine, happy to hear his voice sliding over her. Her mouth curved. 'They'll get used to you.'

'They don't have a choice,' Will stated, his tone resolute. 'It's either my way or the highway.'

'So you're a dictator?' Lu teased, and then bit her lip. Lord, what was she saying? She didn't know him nearly well enough to tease him!

'Only in my job. I know what I want and exactly how I intend to get it.'

So sure, so confident. She wished she could rub herself against him and have some of that innate self-assuredness rub off on her. Oh, hell, forget anything else, she just wanted to rub up against him, full-stop.

He set her nerve-endings on fire... *This is why you shouldn't go so long between dates, Sheppard! When your hormones are invited to a party they head straight for the tequilas and start doing the Macarena.*

'Well, I'll be rooting for you,' Lu said, after a longer than normal silence.

'Thanks,' Will replied. 'It's nearly seven. I've been here since six this morning. Any ideas for where I can eat? I can't face Room Service or takeout.'

'Are you going to live in that hotel for three months?' Lu asked.

'Hell, no. I need to find a flat I can rent, but I haven't had any time. I'm planning to look around on the weekend.'

'So...restaurants. What do you feel like eating?'

'Mac and cheese,' Will responded promptly.

'Mac and cheese, huh?' Lu looked towards the kitchen that sat at the other end of her open-plan lounge. Did she dare? What if he said no? She was mad. Of course he'd say no. But there was a chance—a numpty billion-to-one chance—that he might say yes.

And, because her mother had raised her right, she should do something to say thank you. *Yeah, keep telling yourself that's the reason you are about to invite him over. You might convince yourself in a millennia...or two.*

Pull on your brave girl panties, Sheppard.

'If you're interested, I can do one better than mac and cheese. I have a lasagne that I made and froze. I can whip up a salad to go with it if you...well, don't feel obligated...but I feel like dinner is the least I can do for you since you... Um...you'd probably prefer to eat out,' Lu stammered.

'Lu?'

'Mmm? Yes?' He was going to blow her off. She just knew it.

'Homemade lasagne sounds really great.'

'Ah...OK. Good.' Lu closed her eyes. *Eek!* Now she would actually have to defrost the lasagne and make a salad. And have a shower and do something with her hair...

'I could be there in half an hour? That work for you?'

'Sure.' She'd prefer an hour to primp, but that wasn't going to happen. Well, as per usual, make-up would be sacrificed.

'Do you remember how to get here?' she asked, almost reluctant to let him disconnect even though she'd see him soon.

'I have a pretty good sense of direction, but keep your phone close in case I go off course,' Will told her. 'What is Lu short for, by the way?'

'Um...don't laugh.' Lu blushed. 'Tallulah.'

'Tallulah?'

His tongue caressed her name and Lu shivered.

'Lu suits you better. See you soon.'

As Will pushed the button on the intercom outside Lu's closed gate he thought that the heat and humidity of Durban were obviously frying his brain. What did he think he was going to achieve from this visit apart from, obviously, some homemade pasta? Lu had crossed his mind more than once over the last few days but he'd be lying if he said it was only because he was worried about her, worried that the date-rape drug might have had a side effect that neither of them, nor the hospital doctors, knew about. He'd been thinking about *her* and, unusually, not just as someone he wanted to get into bed.

'Why don't you try being friends with a woman instead?'

Kelby's words from last week kept popping in and out of his head, quickly followed by a flash of Lu's freckled face, her sea-coloured eyes. For the first time in for ever he could see himself being friends with a woman—being friends with Lu. Sure, he was attracted to her. But from the little he'd seen of her he really liked her as well. She seemed unconcerned about who he was and what he did.

She was, he decided, refreshing.

He was in a new country, trying out a new type of job. Maybe he should try something different when it came to the opposite sex too.

Will felt himself relaxing as her gate rolled open and he steered the SUV up the long driveway. *A change is as good as a holiday*, he thought, pulling to a stop.

Then why did his heart thump when he saw her standing by the open front door, dressed in a similar outfit to the one she'd changed into in his hotel room—a pair of white cotton shorts and a teal tank top with thin straps that showed off an inch of her flat belly? He lifted his hand as he left the car and patted two dogs of indeterminate breed, sliding a hot glance at those long, tanned legs and bare feet tipped with fire red toenails.

Friends. New approach. Don't let your libido distract you. It had, as he well remembered, led him into far too much trouble before.

'Hi.' Lu lifted her glass. 'I started without you. Want one?'

'Hi, back.' Will waved the bottle he held in his hand as he walked up the two stone steps to the door. He brushed past a pot plant and his nose was filled with the scent of sweet lemons. The bigger of the dogs nudged his hand and Lu grinned. 'Harry, stop it!'

'Harry?'

'Potter's behind you. The cat's are Dumbel and Dore.'

Nice place, Will thought as he stepped into a huge hall and Lu closed the door behind him. She took the bottle he held out. He searched her face, happy to see some colour in her cheeks, less blue under her eyes. Lu dropped her eyes from his and Will looked around. A coat rack stood next to the door and a large antique credenza squatted next to the wall, photographs in silver frames crowding its surface. A massive vase of haphazard flowers stood on a narrow high table, and the wall in front of him was dominated by two over-sized canvas photographs of two young boys, their faces a chocolate smear.

'My brothers,' Lu explained as he stepped up to look at the photographs. 'Come through this way. I thought we'd eat on the veranda.'

Will followed Lu through a huge kitchen and his mouth started to water at the smell of garlicky, herby, meaty pasta. The kitchen flowed into a large, messy lounge with battered leather couches, a laptop on a big coffee table and a large screen television. Over-sized glass and wooden doors led onto a wraparound veranda, which had its own set of couches, a casual dining table and an incredible view over the city to the Indian Ocean.

'I want to live here,' Will muttered, placing the bottle on the table and dropping his mobile and keys next to it.

'Yeah, the view is pretty impressive.' Lu deftly poured wine into the empty glass on the table and handed it over.

Will sat down in the closest chair and tried to ignore the buzz in his pants when Lu sat down opposite him and folded her legs up under her butt. He pulled his eyes from that expanse of bare leg, looked around and liked what he saw. The house was huge, filled with old, once expensive furniture and eclectic art.

'I love your house,' Will said, after sipping his wine. 'I'm crazy about buildings. Built in the thirties?'

'1931 and inspired by the times: Art Deco rules. It was my grandparents' and then my father's,' Lu explained. 'My grandmother did all the stained-glass panels above the windows and next to the front door. My grandfather collected the furniture.'

He'd noticed the furniture on his walk-through, and now glanced through the open veranda doors into the lounge. He saw another set of canvas photographs: black and white, like the others in the hall, and brimming with emotion and energy. 'Mind if I take a look?'

Lu shrugged. 'Go ahead.'

The first canvas was of a fantastically, lushly beautiful woman, dressed in a corset and fishnet stockings, a walking cane across her ample chest. She had more curves than a mountain pass and, while her face was partially covered by the brim of a top hat, her expression radiated fun and excitement and raw sensuality.

He moved to the other photograph: a long, lanky man, lying in a hammock, a beer bottle in his hand and his eyes—Lu's eyes—half closed. A golfing magazine lay face-down on his stomach.

Sexy, successful, attractive. Everything she wasn't right now, Lu thought as she watched Will take a closer look at the photographs.

Everything she'd ever wanted to be but didn't know how. The embodiment of what a successful life looked like.

His looks were an added bonus, she thought, but his success and the material wealth that came along with it was all his own, created by hard work. *His* hard work and dedication. How she envied him that—envied the fact that whatever he had, and she knew it was a lot, he could say that he'd earned it. Unlike her every possession, including her photography equipment, which came from the massive inheritance her parents had left behind.

An inheritance that would have been non-existent if her parents had died a couple of weeks later than they had. It had been a standard joke between them that there were many millions of reasons to bump the other off...and it was fascinatingly ironic that they'd died together, victims of an out-of-control articulated vehicle.

If they'd lived this house would have been a distant memory for her—sold to pay off the overdraft, the credit cards, the personal loans. At the time of their death they'd been, as Lu had later discovered, living on fresh air and the last couple of thousand on her father's credit cards. The car and credit card payments hadn't been made in months; the utilities bills had been late.

Sorting through the financial mess had been a nightmare on top of the horror of losing them. It was probably the biggest secret she'd kept from the twins: that they wouldn't be enjoying such a privileged lifestyle if their parents had lived.

But her parents' secret remained exactly that; she'd never told a living soul and would never tell the twins. One person feeling guilty and conflicted about the lifestyle of their family was enough. She didn't need to burden them with that information; it was, as she well knew, a heavy load to carry.

The flip and very selfish side of that coin was that if her parents *were* still around they might not have anything like the material wealth surrounding them now, but she'd be supporting herself—working...contributing. She would be on a career path, settled and established. Maybe not rich, like Will, but comfortable, secure. Fulfilled because her security came from the sweat of her own brow and not because her parents had rushed off to a meeting with their bank manager and ended up under the chassis of a ten-ton truck.

So she was ten years behind? It wasn't as if she was old and past her prime. She was young and fit and determined...and she had time. So what if most women her age were thinking about moving onto the next stage of their lives—marriage and babies? That was their life, not hers.

She'd catch up...she *had* to. In the couple of weeks

since the boys had left she'd been clubbing—she was deliberately ignoring the issue of the spiked drink—she'd worked on her website, sorted out her studio and looked into dance classes.

She'd even invited a man around for dinner.

That was progress, wasn't it?

Will walked back onto the veranda and leaned against the balcony. 'Your parents?'

Lu nodded and sipped her wine. 'My mother was a cabaret artiste and performer, my father a golf pro.'

'Was?'

'They're dead. Car accident. Ten years ago,' Lu said in a monotone, and she didn't know that pain flickered in and out of her eyes.

Will winced. 'Damn, I'm sorry about that. Did you take the photos?'

Lu nodded. 'I took them shortly before they died; they were supposed to be used in an assignment I had due.'

Lu steeled herself. He'd ask about their death now; people always wanted to know the details.

'And is photography your passion? Your business?'

When Lu recovered from her surprise at his change of subject she focused on the question. Her passion? Absolutely. Her business? She didn't know. Could she even call herself a photographer? She didn't have much of a reputation, didn't have that much of a portfolio, and hardly any experience. Did updating her website and looking for new business mean that she was actually *in* business?

Well, she wasn't a pseudo-mommy any more, so maybe she was.

She touched a camera that sat on the table next to her. 'I always have one close by so I suppose it must be. Is rugby yours?'

'My passion and my business? Absolutely.'

Will placed his ankle on his knee and Lu wondered why he made her skin prickle. Her veranda was spacious, but he made it seem smaller, cosier. Lu tried to put her finger on what he made her feel. *Alive*, she realised with a shock.

He made her feel alive. And that she mattered.

Dangerous thoughts, Lu, you need to switch gears. What had they been talking about? Rugby...

Lu's eyes shot up, sharpened and collided with his. 'Oh, and on the subject of photography and rugby, who took that photo of you for the Rays' webpage?'

'You looked up our webpage?' Will asked, his mouth twitching with amusement.

Lu blushed, caught out. 'I was...it just popped up.' Oh, she was such a rotten liar. 'Anyway...that photo of you? Who took it?'

'What's wrong with the photo?' he asked, amused at her indignation.

'What's *right* with it? It's shocking! The light is wrong, there are shadows, you look older than you are...exhausted. Geez, a ten-year-old with a point-and-shoot could've done a better job,' Lu stated, her embarrassment and awkwardness temporarily banished as she spoke about her work.

'Photography is *so* your passion. Why do you doubt it?'

Lu blinked at him, nonplussed as she thought about

his question. Because right now she doubted every-thing about herself.

Will saved her from making a coherent reply when he continued in his smooth, deep voice, 'Think you can do better?'

Lu's eyes sparked with indignation. 'I *know* I can do better.'

Lu didn't pick up the tongue Will placed in his cheek. 'I think the photographer was one of the most reputable in Durban.'

'Well, I'd demand a refund.' Lu sniffed. 'Shoddy work.'

Will gestured to the camera with his wine glass. 'Prove it.'

'What?'

'I'm a tough subject—the least photogenic person in the world.'

That was like saying that Ryan Reynolds wasn't sexy. 'You?'

'Why do you think I keep endorsement deals and modelling work to a minimum? I suck at camera work.' Will motioned to the camera. 'Do your worst. Actually, do your best. Take a photo of me that's better than the one on the website; God knows I need it.'

Lu narrowed her eyes at him and couldn't resist the challenge in his eyes. Without breaking his stare she reached for her camera, flipped it on by touch and lifted it to her face. She adjusted the light filters, the focus, and fiddled with the settings, and then her fin-ger was on the button and his image flew to the mem-ory card.

There was so much she was unsure of but this she

knew. Lighting, framing, capturing, Lu slid into the zone. She knew how to pull an image together, to capture the light on his face, the glint in his eyes, the tiny dimple in his cheek.

She might not know him, but through her camera she caught a glimpse of his soul.

And somehow, very strangely, she felt that she recognised it.

FOUR

—

'I can't believe this photo.' Will picked up her camera from the table and looked at his image captured in the viewfinder. 'It's really good. I look serious, but approachable.'

Will expected her to say *I told you so*, but she just winged a quick, grateful smile his way as she placed a huge bowl of salad on the table.

Will pulled on his shirt and left his towel wrapped around his hips so that it could soak up the water from the still dripping board shorts she'd found for him to wear. Lu had suggested he take a swim while she got dinner on the table, and since it was muggy and hot he'd quickly agreed.

He gestured to the colourful cushions on the chairs. 'I'm wet.'

'Yours won't be the first wet bum to sit there,' Lu told him, dipping a serving spoon into the lasagne. Behind her back both dogs climbed up onto separate chairs and snuggled into the plump cushions. Lu heard their contented huffs and shook her head.

'You're very relaxed about your house,' Will commented, thinking that his two sisters would have had a hissy fit by now at the thought of dogs on their furniture.

'The furniture is old and the animals are as much a part of this family as we are.'

Will sat down, topped up their glasses with wine and pushed his wet hair back from his forehead. He skimmed a glance over her face as she reached for a plate to dish up onto and wondered what was going on in that very busy head of hers. Not that he cared, he assured himself, he was just being naturally curious.

Will took the plate she held out, put it down in front of him and reached for the salad. He actually groaned his approval as he dumped a mountain on his plate. 'God, this looks so good.'

'Tuck in,' Lu told him as she dished up her own food.

They ate in silence for a couple of minutes—well, she ate and Will inhaled his food. Even at home he wasn't much of a cook, so he mostly ate out or ordered take out, and he'd forgotten the pleasure of a simple home-cooked meal. It reminded him of his family, of feeling relaxed, content.

When his immediate hunger was satisfied Will slowed down and in between bites sipped his wine. Over Lu's head he could see the portraits of her parents, and he frowned as a thought occurred to him.

'So, you have brothers, right? Where are they?'

'They left for university a couple of weeks ago. They're in Cape Town.'

Curiosity turned to intrigue. 'And did you see much of them over the past decade?'

'Sometimes far too much of them.'

Lu's smile bloomed and his heart flip-flopped.

'I became their guardian. We all lived here together.'

Will lowered his wine glass in shock. 'You took on twin boys when you were—how old were you?'

'I'd just turned nineteen.'

'And they were—what?—eight?'

'Thereabouts.'

'But...you were just a baby yourself. They *allowed* you to do that?'

Lu shrugged. 'There wasn't anybody else who could take them, and I sure as hell wasn't going to put them into care so that I could carry on with my life.'

Will watched her eat as he thought about what *he'd* been doing when he was nineteen. Playing first-class rugby in England, pretending to study, chasing girls, drinking, having a ball. Her sacrifice took his breath away.

'But—'

Lu lifted her hand and he instantly cut off his question.

'It's a bit of a scratchy subject with me at the moment. Do you mind if we don't talk about it?'

'No, that's fine.' It wasn't, of course. He wanted to shove aside those curtains in her eyes and see what she was hiding, thinking...feeling. Unusual, since he never delved deeper than just below the surface; he'd never needed to.

Will cleared his plate and looked at her bent head. If this was any other girl he'd call on years of practice, find a dozen innocuous topics to discuss, but he was finding that he didn't want to skim the surface with Lu. How could he? She'd reluctantly told him about the death of her parents, that she'd raised her twin brothers. And, more unusually, she didn't want to talk about her past... Most women would have given him a blow-by-blow account of her life by now.

She was different, Will thought. And original. And because she was so different he wasn't quite sure how to handle her.

But they couldn't sit here in this awkward silence. He'd have to say something.

'So, do you read?' she asked, at exactly the same time that he asked how often she went clubbing. 'You're kidding, right?' Lu shook her head. 'That was the first time in...um...six, seven—eight?—years. I'd rather hand-wash sweaty rugby kit than go again.'

'That bad, huh? But if you hated it so much why were you there?'

Lu wrinkled her nose in annoyance. 'My brothers.'

Will looked at the lasagne dish and Lu immediately passed it over. He gestured for her to continue explaining.

She sat back in her chair and stared at her plate for a long time. When she lifted her eyes again they were shuttered and guileless. 'It was just a stupid dare between us.'

Will narrowed his eyes at the lie. Why would going to a nightclub be a dare for an adult woman? Nope, there was a lot more to that story than she was saying.

'If that was the best dare they could come up with then they are very uncreative.' Will deliberately kept his voice mild.

Her blush told him that she realised he'd caught her lie. Lu licked her lips and took a sip of her wine as he placed his utensils together on the plate and pushed it away.

'More?'

Will groaned. 'No, I'm stuffed. It was good, thanks. Do you always keep trays of lasagne in your freezer?'

Lu's wide smile flashed. 'With teenage boys in the house you always need extra food for when their mates come home unexpectedly. And I keep a couple of trays in the freezer for Mak to take when he runs out of food—which is often.'

Mak again. Will was very rarely jealous. Clothes and looks didn't concern him, and his success at whatever he chose to do was his to achieve or not, so he never felt envy. However, he did feel something distantly related to jealousy at the very apparent bond Lu shared with Mak.

Will swallowed the last of his wine and thought that if he was at the point of admitting jealousy and frustration then it was definitely time for him to go. He deliberately looked at his watch and was surprised to find that it was later than he'd suspected. 'I should go. We have a gruelling early-morning team run along the beach tomorrow.'

Lu stood up with him. 'You run with the team?'

'I can't expect them to do anything I won't do,' Will replied, picking up their plates and the lasagne dish. 'In the kitchen?'

'Thanks. I'll stack them in the dishwasher.'

Lu fiddled with her camera, then picked up their wine glasses and the salad bowl and followed him inside.

Will changed from the swimming shorts into his

clothes and thought that in his normal life, with a 'normal' girl, he'd just lay it on the line and suggest they spend the night together: big fun, no commitment. That spark of attraction to Lu was there, he admitted to himself. It burned hard and bright and he'd ignored it all night. Whenever he thought about acting on it something held him back.

His conversation the other night with Kelby kept resonating with him and he was forced to admit that Kelby had been bang-on with a lot of his observations. He was Mr Control these days—his life went into a tailspin when he cut loose—and if he had to be totally truthful he admitted that he'd never allowed any of the attraction he felt to a woman to be fanned into a fire. He used sexual attraction to get...well, *sex*. And while he always made sure that both he and his partner had a fun time in bed, he knew that at any time he could walk away. He didn't allow himself to get emotionally involved because he genuinely believed that he couldn't offer a woman anything permanent. Every fire went out eventually.

Yet Kelby's question kept prodding him in the head. *'Why don't you try being friends with a woman instead?'*

And Lu—strong, calm and capable—was just the type of woman he could be friends with. Her decision to raise her twin brothers at such a young age told him that she was loyal and determined. He liked those traits in men and they were very attractive in a woman too. He could respect her—another trait he considered essential for a friendship.

And, with her lithe body and quick smile, she was a lot easier on the eye than Kelby and his other mates.

Lu had just started to stack the dishwasher when Will walked back into the room, his car keys dangling from his fingers. 'Thanks, Lu. For dinner and the company.'

'Pleasure.' Lu walked him to the hall and shoved her hand into the pocket of her shorts, pulling out a memory card. She held it between her fingers. 'Change the photo, OK?'

Will's smile was warm and deep as he took the card. 'I'll pass it along. Thank you.'

Will couldn't stop himself from lifting up his hand to touch her cheek. He needed to know whether her skin was as soft as it looked, whether her bottom lip was a plump as he thought it was.

It was all that and more.

Will shook his head as he turned away. He'd never had the urge to touch his mates' faces and thank God. If he did he'd get the snot smacked out of him.

Lu looked up as Mak and Deon walked into her kitchen, courtesy of the set of keys Mak had been given by her father all those years ago, when they'd first become friends. Lu accepted a hug from Mak's high-functioning Down Syndrome son and smiled when Deon headed straight for her cookie jar. He was as at home in her house as the twins were. Lu had been his official babysitter since his mother had left a year after his birth, shortly before her parents' death.

Mak took a seat at the kitchen counter and accepted the glass of iced tea Lu pushed across. 'No wine?'

'It's three in the afternoon, Mak. A bit early.'

'Damn.'

'Tough day?' Lu asked, knowing that it was a battle for Mak to juggle his business and the demands and needs of a highly active special needs child. Deon had an *au-pair* he adored, and numerous aunts and uncle who showered him with attention but Mak was his lifeline, his safety net, his hero.

'How did the interview go at that other school?'

Mak shrugged. 'Fine. They'd take him tomorrow if I wanted, but I'm holding out for St Clare's.'

'You haven't heard yet?'

Mak looked frustrated. 'No.'

Lu bit the inside of her lip. Deon was lonely and needed to get back into school—a school where, unlike at the last one, he wouldn't be incessantly bullied and tormented.

Mak waved his hand in the air. 'I should hear within a couple of weeks. So, have you had any luck picking up work?'

Lu blew air into her cheeks. 'Not a damn thing! I've only had one enquiry on the website and I've visited all the bridal shops and florists and dished out my card, hoping for referrals. I'm thinking of getting another job—'

'Lu, it's only been a month since the boys left. Give yourself some time. Keep plugging at it. Something will come up. So...I saw Will Scott's flashy Range Rover parked in your driveway the other night.'

'Were you spying on me again?' Lu demanded.

'Sure. That's what good friends do,' Mak replied.

'I came around to check on you and saw Will's car, so I left.'

'You should've joined us.'

'And have Deon buzzing on rugby talk for the next week? No, thanks!'

Lu smiled. Deon was completely rugby-obsessed and the Rays were his idols. He would be thoroughly over-excited if he met Will, and he'd nag Mak and her to make Will introduce him to the rest of the team. When Deon got a notion in his head it required a water cannon to dislodge it.

Lu explained that she'd invited Will around for supper to say thank you.

Mak took a sip of his drink. 'So, did he come around to say it was a pleasure to your thank you? Or did he have other pleasure on his mind?' Mak waggled his eyebrows at her.

Lu glowered at him. 'It wasn't like that, Mak!'

'It's *always* like that, Lu.'

Lu didn't tell him about Will touching her face, about the flare of passion she'd thought she saw in his eyes. She placed her elbows on the counter and grinned at Mak. 'He *is* hot, though.'

Make rolled his eyes. 'So I'm told.'

'So, last night I went to the Botanic Gardens and the Philharmonic Orchestra was playing. I thought that it would be so much fun to have someone to do things with. I mean, I didn't mind being on my own, but—'

Mak looked horrified. 'I am *not* going to any classical concerts.'

Lu laughed. 'Actually, I wasn't thinking about you...

this time. I was kind of considering whether to invite Will along the next time. Do you think I could do that?'

'Women have been asking men out for a while now,' Mak pointed out.

Lu slid her bum onto a stool. 'Do you know what I realised this week, Mak?'

'What, honey?'

'That I have been so worried about the boys being independent enough, strong enough to go off on their own, and they are fine. Me—not so much. Of the three of us *I'm* the one who isn't independent. *I'm* the one having the most problems adjusting. Apart from that night with Will I've hated being in this house alone, waking up alone, going to sleep alone. The lack of noise, the tidiness... I miss them so damn much.'

'Of course you do.'

'I desperately need to work, to prove to myself that I am something other than a fake mommy. I want to create again. I want people's eyes to react—good or bad—when then see my photos. I miss it, Mak. I miss being...*productive*. I can take as many photos of the sea, of the dogs, as I want, but it's not the same as creating images for someone else. I miss being...*me*.'

Mak listened and waited for Lu to carry on.

'And...I guess I'm just lonely. I never realised I was until the boys left. Having supper with Will the other night made me realise how much I've missed being with someone...and, sorry, you don't count.'

'You're too skinny and too pale for me anyway.'

Lu reached across the counter to swat his shoulder. 'I thought that Will would be an ideal man to prac-tise on.'

Mak's head snapped up. 'Huh? What?'

'I can use him to get my confidence back, to get back into the whole dating dance again. To help me be-come—independent. Is that the word I'm looking for?'

'You are making absolutely no sense.'

'I've lost the ability—I'm not even sure I ever *had* the ability—to flirt, to enjoy a man's company, to do the dance. Having a flirtation, a fling with Will, would boost my confidence and in a weird way sort of be a... um...a kick start to this new phase of my life. A way to remind myself that I'm more than what I was—some-thing other than the being the twins' guardian, their housekeeper, their taxi.'

Would Mak understand that she suddenly felt lost and unable to cope now that there was only herself to worry about? She was supposed to feel relieved and free. Instead she felt more insecure and scared than ever before.

That wasn't right. Or fair. And it definitely wasn't acceptable. So she'd do something about it.

Preferably with Will. Could she do it? Was she brave enough?

Mak was quiet for a long time. 'I'm all for you hav-ing some fun—getting your groove back. But there are dangers in this, Lu.'

'Like?'

'You falling for him and getting hurt, for one.'

Lu shook her head. 'Firstly, he's avoided serious re-lationships for years, and even if I didn't know that he has "No Trespassing" signs all over his heart, so I know that falling for him would be stupid. Secondly, he's only here for three months—less than that now.

That's strike number two. He'll be my practice man and when he leaves I'll be fine. I just need someone who's *kind of* in my life to ease me into the rest of my life. Does that make any sense at all?'

'Sort of. If you manage to keep it just fun and games.'

'I won't allow myself to get attached to him.'

'Sometimes you can't help it,' Mak insisted.

'Mak, it's just an idea, and if he says no then it's no harm, no foul. As grateful as I am to him rescuing me from the club, I have no intention of trailing after him, dragging my tongue on the floor, appreciative of any attention he'll give me. I won't beg, I still have my pride. And if he says yes then I'll keep my emotional distance.'

'Mmm. Not sure if you have ever been able to do that, Lu.' Mak stood up and rested his hands on her bare shoulders. He pulled her in for a hug. 'And, talking about clubbing, I am so very, very sorry about the other night, Lu. God, I lie awake thinking...'

Lu shook her head. 'Don't Mak. I'm fine.'

'You're fine because someone else was looking out for you.' Mak rested his chin on the top of her head. 'Your dad would have had my head.'

'I'm a big girl, Mak; I've been looking after myself and the twins for a long time,' Lu told him. 'I don't need you to look after me. I'm taking charge of my life, getting used to being on my own. I've got to get my head, my life, together. I can do it, Mak!'

Mak grinned down at her determined face. 'May I point out that the only person in this room who sounds doubtful about that is *you*, sweetheart?'

'It's taking some practice,' Lu admitted.

'It always does.' Mak stepped away from her and reached across the counter for her mobile. 'So, call him.'

Lu yelped. 'Not now! Um…I need to think about what we can do together.'

'I have double tickets to a cooking demo by that celebrity pastry chef you're so gaga about.'

'Rupert Walker?' Lu squealed. *Oh, wow!* She'd casually mentioned to Mak that she'd like to see the demo, and Mak, good mate that he was, had arranged tickets.

'I was going to go with you, but I think you should take Will. You can torture him instead.'

'I don't think it's his thing. But I'd love to go.' Lu's eyes widened as Mak scrolled through the numbers on her phone, pushed the green button and handed it to her.

'It's ringing. Ask him.'

'Makhosi, you son of a…! What am I supposed…?' Mak thrust the phone in her direction and the next moment Will's deep voice had her toes curling.

'Hey, Lu. What's up?'

'Um…hi. Feel free to say no, because I certainly don't expect you to say yes—'

Will laughed. 'That sounds ominous.'

Lu glared at Mak, who was rolling his finger silently to tell her to get on with it.

'I was given tickets for a celebrity baking demo on Monday night and I was wondering if you'd like to go with me.' Lu expelled the words in a whoosh. She pictured herself jumping into a cavernous pool and finding it empty of water. *Splat!*

'Ah...um...it's really not my thing...but OK. Shall I pick you up?'

Oh, dear Lord, there was water in the pool and she was floating. *Yay!*

Lu pulled a tongue at Mak's satisfied face as they made arrangements. Turning away from his smirky expression she allowed a broad smile to cross her face.

I am woman, hear me roar, she thought. Well, it wasn't quite a roar but it was definitely more than a whimper. *Go me!*

An hour later Lu pulled her SUV into an empty space in the parking lot of the Stingrays' Rugby Union corporate offices. She'd been about to end her conversation with Will when he'd told her he was with Kelby Cotter, the Rays' CEO, and that he wanted to have a word. Kelby had asked her to meet with him to discuss a photography project she might be interested in. *Might* be interested? She *itched* to pick up her camera and get to work!

At this moment she'd walk into the fires of hell if there was photography work there, and any project that had the Rays' name attached to it would be a huge boost to her non-existent career.

Lu got out of the car and looked down at her short black skirt, her tangerine T-shirt and slightly scuffed wedges, and wondered if she should have splurged on another, more businesslike outfit. Heavy silver bracelets ran up her arm and ethnic silver earrings hung halfway to her shoulders. She'd forgotten to put on make-up. Lu sighed. She'd meant to but, as per normal, it had slipped her mind.

Lu was directed to the PR executive's office by a receptionist who looked like a high-class model. Perfect hair, perfect nails...super-slim. Lu resisted the urge to wipe her clammy hands on her skirt and again wondered why she was being shown to an office in the PR and Publicity Department.

She readjusted the strap of her shoulder bag and knocked on the door. Two seconds later a large, rugged teddy bear of a man opened the door and smiled down at her. He held a sandwich in one hand and shrugged his apologies.

'Lu? Sorry—first moment I've had free to eat lunch,' he explained. 'Kelby Cotter.'

He raised the half-sandwich for another bite and gestured Lu to a seat in front of a very feminine, very messy desk. He swallowed his last bite, took a swig of water from the bottle on his desk and scrabbled amongst the papers.

'Got it.' Kelby flicked the memory card from her camera at her and Lu snapped it out of the air. 'Amazing photos of Will. Can I have them?'

Surely he could have asked her over the phone whether he could use them? She should ask him to pay for them. Her brain whirled. But if she gave them to him and asked for the credit then that would help to raise her profile. 'Uh...sure.'

Kelby tipped his head at her and let out a rumbling laugh. 'You can't just give your work away, Lu!'

'So you'll buy them from me?'

Kelby named a figure that had Lu's eyes widening. It seemed that the Rays paid their photographers very well indeed.

Emboldened by his kind eyes, Lu asked why the CEO was dealing with publicity and PR issues.

'Fair question. My head of PR flew to Cape Town to be with her terminally ill mother. I'm overseeing the department until she returns, and it's easier to work in her office than move all her stuff to mine.' Kelby leaned back in his chair and folded his hands across his portly stomach. 'I have two other offers for you. Both of them involve you getting paid.'

Lu blushed and felt like an idiot. And excited. And nervous if these projects had anything to do with Will Scott. 'OK. That sounds interesting.'

'I browsed through the other photos on the media card Will gave me and I was blown away by some of your images. They are utterly fantastic.'

'Thank you,' Lu said, her brain racing to remember what images he was talking about. Some photos of the twins and their friends, the baby photo shoot, some beach scenes.

'My partner and I have a six-month-old daughter and we'd love some photographs. Some portrait shots of her and some informal shots of the three of us.'

Yay! A job. 'That's very doable. I have a studio at home with all the props, backdrops and lighting. As for the informal shots, we can do them at your home—whenever it's convenient.'

'Uh...we live in a rather cramped loft at the moment, while our house is being built, so that wouldn't work.' Kelby fiddled with his pen. 'Will says you have a beautiful garden...can we do them there? It'll have to be on a Sunday. I'm swamped during the week.'

'Sure. What about this Sunday morning?'

'Fantastic!' Kelby looked up at a sharp rap on his door. 'Will! She said yes to doing Micki's photos! We're going to do them on Sunday morning at her house.'

'Told you she would.'

Lu's stomach swooped and rolled as she turned in her chair. Dressed in a pair of black athletic shorts, an untucked blue Rays branded T-shirt and trainers, he looked fit and sexy, his hair damp as if he'd just come out of a shower. Will stepped into the room and Lu's eyes widened as he dropped his head to kiss her cheek. Because she pulled back—in surprise—his kiss landed on her temple. Will stood up and his eyes connected with hers. He'd clocked her surprise and those fabulous topaz eyes glinted with amusement.

Will perched himself on the corner of the desk and helped himself to the other half of Kelby's sandwich.

'Hey!' Kelby protested.

'Didn't Angie put you on a diet? No carbs? Salad only?' Will demanded in between bites. 'I'm stopping you from getting into trouble with your woman, man.'

'But I'm starving!'

'Have a carrot stick or come run with me. Then you can eat shrimp and mayo sandwiches.' Will wiped his mouth with a serviette he'd found next to the sandwich. 'Or get your lard-ass back to the gym.'

'Like I have time for that,' Kelby grumbled.

Will waved the sandwich in Lu's direction. 'Have you asked her yet?'

'I was interrupted by my annoying head coach,' Kelby said, looking longingly at the empty plastic sandwich container. He turned to Lu and his eyes were serious. 'I'm looking for a contracted photographer to work for the Rays—capturing official images of the squad for us to use for various promotional campaigns. I don't have the time to phone around looking for free-lance photographers who cost the earth even if they are available. I need *you* to be the official Rays photographer.'

Lu looked from Kelby to Will and realised that neither of them were laughing, so it couldn't be a joke. She thought she'd make doubly sure. 'Sorry—are you being serious?' she asked, her heart racing.

'Yep. You'd have to work flexible hours—work with me, work with the guys.' He sent her a dubious look. 'Can you handle twenty-plus men at a time?'

'She raised twin boys. She's pretty much Super-woman,' Will stated calmly, and Lu shot him a quick grin and tried not to blush at his compliment.

Lu looked at Kelby. 'Wow. Sorry, this is quite over-whelming. Are you sure?'

'If you give me images half as good as the ones on that card I'll be a happy man.'

Lu raised her chin in determination. 'They'll be as good or better.'

Kelby looked at Will and nodded. 'I like her.'

'I thought you would,' he said, and Lu's heart flopped against her ribs.

Kelby's ringing mobile phone broke their look and, after telling his caller that he'd phone him back in five minutes, Kelby reached for a file on his desk. He handed Lu some papers and stood up. 'Look that contract over and start on Monday.' He waved his mobile. 'Sorry, I have to sort something out.'

'Thank you so much.'

Lu noticed Kelby's eyes sliding to his desk drawer and saw that Will had caught the action too.

'What are you hiding, Kelby?' he demanded. Will stood up and walked around the desk, yanked open a drawer. He shook his head as he pulled out an oil stained packet. 'Jelly doughnuts? Seriously? With *your* stress levels and lack of exercise?'

Kelby groaned. 'Who are you? The food police?'

Will opened the packet, pulled one out and bit down. 'These are good.' He looked at Lu and waved the doughnut in the air. 'Want some?'

Lu shook her head. 'No thanks.'

'I hate you so much, Scott. I'll be back in five minutes,' Kelby muttered, looking utterly bereft. 'So are we on for Sunday, Lu.'

Lu felt sorry for him. Being on a diet was the pits. 'Come at ten—for tea. I'll make you some super-healthy beetroot cupcakes that you'll think are laden with fat and calories.'

Kelby brightened immediately. 'You—I like.' He pointed at Will. 'Him—not so much.'

FIVE

—

Lu swallowed as the door clicked shut and Will resumed his place on the corner of the desk, his knee just inches from hers. He folded his arms across his chest and looked down at her.

He'd thought about her far too much since he'd had supper at her house and had been forcing himself not to call. He'd been surprised by *her* call and even more startled by the relief he'd felt at hearing from her again.

Lu lifted her face and in doing so exposed that fine strip of skin just below her jaw that he wanted to nibble on... He'd spent many nights thinking about her, imagining what he'd do to her if he had her naked and willing. Will gave himself a mental punch to the head.

Lu glanced down at the contract in her hand and he watched as pleasure bloomed in her cheeks. 'I've got a *job*, Will.'

'I know...' He bit his tongue to keep the word *honey* from slipping out. 'Congratulations.'

'I've got to tell the boys.'

Lu shot him an enormous smile before picking

up her bag. Dumping it on the desk next to him, she stood up to scrabble in it and eventually yanked out her mobile. Will heard the rumble of a male voice as he stretched out his legs and crossed his feet.

Will listened patiently as she spoke to one brother and then the other and then, sending him an apologetic look, quickly ran through the news again with Mak. Every time she said the words 'official photographer' she did a hip wiggle that had the blood rushing from his head.

Attraction aside, he was enjoying watching Lu bounce out of her shoes with excitement. When had she last had momentous news of her own to report? He suspected that it had been a long, long time. This was all hers; it had nothing to do with her brothers, Mak or anyone else.

He knew what success felt like—the satisfaction a person felt when the validation of hard work or talent came their way. He'd experienced it most of his life, was probably addicted to it, and had possibly become a bit blasé about his successes. Apart from his 'Stupid Years', failure was rarely—OK, never—an acceptable option.

Lu finished her conversation with Mak and looked up at him, her mermaid eyes excited. 'I'm even deeper in debt to you now. You rescue me *and* you hook me up with a job.'

No, he wasn't going to allow her to shift the credit to him or anyone else. This was her moment. 'All I did was hand Kelby the media card. I didn't say or do anything more. You got this job because you obviously have some wicked skills with a camera.'

Lu rocked on her heels. 'So you didn't hint or suggest that he should—?'

'You're assuming that I have a lot more power than I actually do. I wouldn't tolerate anyone telling *me* how to coach, so I extend the same respect to the publicity division. I wouldn't dare tell them how to promote or publicise. No, Lu, *you* did this,' Will told her, his voice low and serious. She needed to understand that this was her achievement and hers alone.

Lu looked at him for a long minute and then her hips shimmied again in excitement. He really wished she wouldn't. How was he expected not to think about what those hips were made for when she did that?

'Yee-hah!' Lu laughed and did a little pirouette. 'So, what time do you think I should be at work on Monday? What should I wear? And, more importantly, how many lenses should I bring? Maybe I should bring all of them—'

Will's lips quirked. 'How many do you have?'

'Eight? Nine?'

He swallowed his laugh. 'I'm sure you won't need them all. And Kelby will e-mail you what you need to know. Or tell you on Sunday. I'm finally going to see if I can find a temporary flat to move into. I can't stand that hotel a minute longer.'

Will moved to stand in front of her, resting his hand on the desk next to her hip. He saw the heat sliding into her cheeks, caught her motion to lift her hand to touch him and felt disappointed when it fell back to her side.

Will moved closer so that his clothes brushed hers. 'Congratulations on your job, Lu.'

'Thanks.'

'Every new job should be celebrated.'

What was he doing? *It's just a kiss,* he told his inner critic. *No big deal.* He'd kissed lots of woman before and walked away unscathed.

Besides, kissing her wasn't a big deal...he could stop at any time.

Yeah, but you've never kissed a mermaid before.

Will placed his hands on her hips, pulled her towards him...and his mouth had barely brushed hers when the office door opened and Kelby bounced inside.

'Whoops!' Kelby exclaimed.

Will looked over his shoulder to see Kelby backtracking and cursed, silently and slow, until the door slammed shut again.

Lu pushed one eyebrow up. 'Well, that was awkward.'

Will bunched his fists to keep from reaching for her again. 'Sorry. That wasn't supposed to happen.'

'You didn't even kiss me properly,' Lu pointed out.

She straightened up and lifted those tanned shoulders. She must have seen something in his face because she stormed into the conversation.

'Will, I don't want this to get weird—especially since I asked you out. I don't want you to think that I'm chasing you, or looking for...' Lu bit her lip as her words trailed off. She waved an agitated hand in the air. 'I'm not looking for anything more than a couple of laughs...some fun. I'm not a complete idiot. I know that you're only going to be around for three months and that was just a little bit of getting carried away by the moment. Frankly, I've just come out of a decade-long relationship with two boys and I gave them every last bit of energy I had. I just want to have some fun—some company. I thought maybe you could do with the same.'

Company? What was she offering? *Company* company or *sex* company? 'Does the company involve getting naked?' he asked in his most prosaic voice.

Judging by the shock that jumped into her eyes, she hadn't reached the bedroom. Damn. Then her eyes smoked over and he knew that she wasn't far behind him. Unfortunately, along with I-want-get-you-naked there was a healthy dose of I-don't-know-what–I'm-doing as well.

And anyway, what was *he* thinking? Hadn't he decided to try something different while he was here in Durban? Yet here he was, sliding right back into old patterns and habit reactions.

'Ah...um...well...' Lu stuttered. *Good God.* 'Actually, I *had* thought about it.' Lu eventually got the words out.

Her expression was calm and composed, slightly challenging. and if her eyes had been sending him the same message he would have had her up against the wall and been kissing the hell out of her by now. Unfortunately she had the most expressive eyes in the world and, thanks to living with two sisters, he easily read the trepidation behind the big girl/brave girl look she was giving him.

OK, I'm scared but I'm prepared to try this anyway.

He wasn't sure why but he instinctively knew that he didn't want to be Lu's experiment.

'Will?'

Knock.

'Will?'

Knock.

'Will!'

Kelby knocked again and Will grinned. Saved by his best friend. Again. He definitely owed Kelby for getting him out of a conversational ass-whipping. Because there was no good way of telling a woman *Thanks, but I'll think about it.*

Will yanked open the door to let Kelby inside and sent Lu what he hoped was a reassuring smile. 'I'll leave you to talk with Kelby and I'll see you on Monday night. OK?'

'Sure.'

Hmm, there was more starch in that one-syllable word than there was in a shed-load of potatoes. Maybe Kelby hadn't saved his ass. He'd just delayed it getting flogged.

Whatcha doing?

That was the third, fourth—fifth?—time one of the twins had texted her today and asked the same question. Lu wished they'd stop worrying so much about her! It was like having two over-protective fathers and, while they were happy about her getting a job, they still weren't relinquishing the idea of her social life.

While Will went to the bar to buy them a drink before the show started Lu quickly snapped a photograph of the billboard advertising the trio of pastry chefs and chocolatiers. Attaching the picture to a message, she sent it to her brothers.

As you can see, I'm out and about.

With a man who very obviously doesn't want to sleep

with me, Lu thought, but she didn't add that. Daniel replied.

Good for you!

Uh...no...and not for the cobwebs either. Nate's response flashed onto her screen.

Apparently not alone. Was Mak serious when he said you're with Will Scott? THE Will Scott? And what is he doing saying yes to a baking demo?

Who knew? Confusion reigned. And Mak had a whale-sized big mouth! Lu texted back.

Yep. And hey! There are tons of celebs here. These chefs are BIG news!

Nate: Bet there aren't any sportsmen there.

Dan: Do you think he could organise for us to meet the squad when we come home?

And when will that be?

When you've taken dance classes, pottery lessons and done a skydive. One date does not a life make.

Yeah! Agreed!

OMG, I'd forgotten how annoying you two can be! :p

Lu shoved her mobile into her bag and looked over to the bar, where Will was easily recognisable in the crush by his broad shoulders in a white shirt worn over a nice pair of jeans. He'd rolled the cuffs back at his wrists and he looked well dressed but casual—relaxed, but as if he'd made a bit of an effort.

And volcano-hot!

She hoped that she'd hit the right note between casual and sexy herself, with a pair of white jeans and a pale green gypsy top falling off one shoulder and belted in at the hips. Strappy heels took her height to

Will's shoulder, yet she still felt—like most people, she supposed—dwarfed by him.

Will walked back towards her and Lu saw various sets of eyes following his progress, noticed the nudging elbows, the behind-the-hand comments. The crowd knew exactly who he was.

'Here you go,' Will said, handing her a glass of wine and hanging on to his tall glass.

How exactly was she supposed to act when she'd hinted that she wouldn't say no to a bedroom invitation and he hadn't say anything? Was that a yes? A no? Hang on, I'll think about it?

What she wouldn't do was let him think that she gave a damn—not even for half a second. She'd learnt to hide her emotions, and pride insisted that she do it now.

'What are you drinking?' Lu asked politely. Look—she could do polite

'Coke. I'm driving. I don't drink that much.'

That hadn't been true in his past, Lu thought. She'd internet-searched him to death and it seemed that at one time Will had had a very unhealthy relationship with alcohol. And dope. And his ex-wife. There had been public fights, public displays of over-the-top affection, busted-up hotel rooms. She couldn't reconcile this controlled, calm man with the younger version of himself she'd read about.

She was pretty sure that younger Will would have slept with her!

'So, did you find a place to rent?' Lu asked as people started moving towards the intimate theatre.

'A flat near you, actually. Practically around the corner. It has a hot tub.'

Oh, good grief. Will in a hot tub...bubbles, champagne... She was not going to think about him skin on skin. He wasn't on the same page as her in terms of skin and sex and... Dear Lord, it was hot in this theatre.

Lu handed their tickets over and pulled in a breath when Will placed his hand on her lower back to guide her down the theatre steps.

'It has a great view,' Will continued as they eventually stopped at the bottom row, dead centre.

Typical Mak to have organised the best seats in the house, Lu thought.

'And it's fully furnished, so I just need to move my clothes across. I'll sign the lease tomorrow. I can also raid your fridge for frozen lasagne when I forget to buy food.'

'I'll make you a tray as a house warming present,' Lu promised him as she sat down. *Maybe.*

'You do love to cook, don't you?' Will shook his head, bemused. 'My skills in the kitchen are limited to making coffee. When you make that tray of lasagne feel free to throw in a couple of those beetroot cupcakes you made for Kelby.'

Lu looked puzzled. 'When did you taste those?'

'You sent some home with Kels and Angie? I ate with them last night.'

'Oh. You liked them, huh?'

'I have a chronic sweet tooth. I'm really hoping that they'll have samples here of what they make tonight.'

Will smiled at her and Lu's stomach flipped over.

His smile should be declared a weapon of mass destruction, she thought. How could she remain irritated when he was so charming? So appealing?

'I love the art of baking...decorating. It's so creative.' Lu sighed. 'I wish I could shoot them as they worked... it would be such fun.'

'Talking of photography—Kelby and Angie were over the moon when they received those first couple of photos of Micki you e-mailed them.'

'Good.' Lu crossed her legs and tapped her finger against the wine glass. 'They are a sweet family. Tell me about yours.'

Affection passed across his face. 'I have two sisters—one in London, one in Wellington—and my folks live in Auckland.'

'Do you miss them?'

'Sure. Although I've lived away from them for so long that it's become normal.'

Lu stared at the stage with its three tables and heaps of cooking equipment and felt her throat constrict. 'The boys are having a fantastic time at uni...I already feel like they're slipping away.

'You are one of my brothers' sporting heroes by the way,' Lu told him as the lights flickered.

'Do they play rugby?'

'And cricket and hockey and soccer. And squash. And they surf... If it's called a sport, they'll try it. The one thing I *don't* miss is ferrying them from activity to activity. Kids here only get their freedom at eighteen, and they've only just got their licences.' Lu stared off into space for a moment. 'That's about the only thing I don't miss about them being gone.'

Will heard the tremor in her voice. 'It's been tough, huh?'

Lu managed a quick laugh and waved his concern away. 'Nah, I'm fine.'

'Tell me the truth, Lu,' Will insisted quietly.

Her irritation with him flooded back with his request. He wanted to get into her head but not into her bed? She knew that she was out of practice dating-wise, but she was pretty sure that her complaint was ass-about-face.

She wanted to tell him that she felt as if she'd had her head amputated, that the house was too quiet and that the dogs were pining. How excited she was to be working again. Instead she just turned her head away and stared at the stage.

'It's starting,' she said as a spotlight highlighted the middle table.

'Who is this dude anyway?' Will demanded in a low whisper.

'Rupert Walker is reputed to be the best baker in the world. And Heinz Martine is an amazing choco-latier and another incredible baker,' Lu whispered as Ruper Walker bounced onto the stage and greeted the audience amongst a flurry of clapping and whistling. 'I don't know the third chef.'

When the audience settled down, the chef, dressed in tartan chef's pants and an enormous maroon chef's hat, put his hands on his hips and looked into the audience.

'Thank you for being here! I always ask for audi-ence help and I usually ask for volunteers, but tonight I understand that Will Scott is in the audience. I'm the biggest, gayest fan!' Rupert shuddered delicately and the audience howled with laughter.

Lu heard Will's groan.

'So maybe Will could come up and give me a hand to make sugar baskets? Will, are you...*game*?'

Will muttered a swear word and looked at Lu with panicked eyes. 'Crap, Lu—I burn bloody water!' he whispered.

As Will stood up Lu slapped her hand against her mouth to keep the laughter from tumbling out.

He bent down so that he spoke directly into her ear. 'You might think this is funny, Mermaid, but I *will* get my revenge.'

Lu's laughter, hot and hard, followed Will up onto the stage.

Will bombed at making sugar baskets. He tried so hard, and was such a good sport about it, but he burnt his sugar twice and accidentally knocked Rupert's elaborate half-finished sugar cage to the floor, where it shattered into a million sugar pieces. Rupert eventually, and very good-naturedly, threw in the towel and sent Will back to his seat, where he proceeded to sit so still that Lu was convinced he'd slept through the rest of the show.

As they cleared the theatre Lu looked up at him and lifted her eyebrows. 'Did you enjoy your sleep?'

'It was great. What did I miss?' Will replied cheerfully.

Lu laughed. 'Nothing you want to know. I, however, learned how to make the ganache for a Sacher Torte.'

Will's eyes lit up. 'That Austrian chocolate cake? Cool—thanks in advance.'

'I'm not making you *that*. It takes hours!'

Will placed his big hand at the base of her neck. 'I'll have one because you laughed at me! When I was called up on stage...when I burnt the sugar—'

Lu gurgled. 'Twice.'

'You were rolling in your seat laughing! Sacher Torte—and if you agree I'll buy you an Irish coffee now.'

Lu grinned as he steered her into the theatre bar. 'Oh, all right, then.'

She followed the waiter to a table that looked out onto the bustling city centre street. Will placed their order and shook his head.

'I get to choose what we do next,' he told her, mock-sternly. 'You can't be trusted.'

Lu lifted one eyebrow, remembered that he wasn't that keen on her, and used the don't-mess-with-me-expression that normally had her brothers wilting. 'You are presuming a lot, aren't you?'

Will sent her a lazy smile. 'You're irritated with me.'

'Are you asking me or telling me?'

'Telling you. You can keep your face blank, Mermaid, but your eyes are far too expressive. You're annoyed because I didn't give you an answer as to whether I wanted to sleep with you or not.'

Bingo! Give the man a gold star!

Will rested his arms on the table and leaned forward. 'Before I respond to that, I need to ask you if you meant what you said in Kelby's office?' Will asked.

Lu frowned. 'Which part?' she asked, wary.

'About not wanting to get involved with anyone?'

'Yes.' She needed to stand on her own feet before

she tried to walk beside someone else. Find out what made her tick, what made her happy.

'OK, so here's what I'm thinking: I can take you to bed—and, yes, I'm alive and breathing, and you're hot, so God knows I want to—and we'll sleep together and have a lot of fun. But I wouldn't see you again. It's not what I do... And that could be weird seeing that we have to work together for the next couple of months.'

'OK...' What was she supposed to say to that? And where was he going with this?

'Or I can *not* take you to bed and see you again.'

Huh?

'Look, Lu, at the risk of sounding like a conceited ass, I can walk into any club in the city and have someone new in my bed every night.'

'You're right—you do sound like a conceited ass,' Lu murmured.

'But I don't have someone to hang with—someone to pass the time with. I enjoy your company...even when you're trying hard to hide your irritation.'

He'd been thinking about it since he'd last seen her—thinking about what Kelby had said. Despite his issues around relationships he genuinely *liked* people and enjoyed being around them. He couldn't foist his after-hours company on his team mates—he was their boss, and who wanted to socialise with their boss? And Kelby had his family and didn't want or need him around. Being single in a foreign city could be lonely, and having someone to hang with would make time go faster, would kill the hours away from the stadium.

Pushing his attraction to her aside—he could do that: he wasn't a hound dog—he genuinely enjoyed her company; she was restful, easy to be with. Lu was real in a way that he hadn't encountered in a woman in long time. When last had he felt so at ease, so relaxed with a woman?

With her, he felt as if he was himself. He curled his lip. Not Will Scott the legendary rugby player. Not the caretaker coach everyone was watching to see what he did with their beloved team. Not Jo Keith's unreliable bad-boy ex-husband.

Just Will. He really liked being just Will.

And he enjoyed the fact that Lu didn't simper or smirk and hang on his every word. That she could call him a conceited ass. Apart from his sisters, who called him far worse, every other woman he'd met only ever complimented him.

It got old very quickly.

He made it sound so easy, so simple, Lu thought. And it *could* be that simple if she didn't overthink this. Sex and walk away, or no sex and a couple of months of hanging together, having fun.

She wanted sex but she *needed* fun. She wanted to laugh like she had earlier, to try new things, to stagger to work bleary-eyed because she'd been out having a blast. She wanted to drink cocktails and wear pretty dresses and try new foods. She wanted to recapture a little of the youth she'd lost, to live life—taste it, feel it, experience it.

And she just knew that she would have more fun with Will than without him.

She'd be mad to pass up this opportunity for one or two nights of hot sex and also—Ding! Ding! Ding!

the jackpot bell rang—her brothers would stop messaging her a hundred times a day to see if she was OK.

'OK—and you'd be helping me out at the same time.'

'That's an added incentive...but how?'

Lu waved her hand in the air—a gesture he now realised she used when she didn't want to pursue a subject. Or when she was trying to be brave.

'Would you consider doing things like pottery lessons? Dance classes?'

'I was thinking about dinner and a movie. But I'd consider anything...*if you gave me a reason.*'

Lu shook her head. 'It's not important and....it's silly.'

'Tell me, Lu.'

She heaved in a huge sigh and stared at the table. 'Before they left for uni my brothers told me that they were worried about me being on my own so much and that they wanted me to start getting out more, start doing stuff. They want me to have some fun, to get out and do things.'

Seeing the flash of misery in her eyes, he reached out to comfort her and allowed himself the rare privilege of stroking his hand down her arm from elbow to wrist. Her bare skin was soft and cool under the pads of his fingers.

'What things?'

'Clubbing was one of them...skydiving, surfing, dance lessons. Pottery classes. A job—but that's sorted.' Lu smiled her thanks at the waiter, who placed their drinks on the table. Irish coffee for her, plain coffee for Will. 'I promised I would. And I have been doing some stuff. But it would be so much more fun if I had someone to do it with.'

Judging by the confusion Will saw in her eyes, he suspected that Lu was dealing with a lot more than she was saying. But her expression begged him not to pursue it.

You have been alone and dealing with far too much for far too long, Mermaid, he told her silently. He knew what that felt like.

Pull it back to the surface, Scott. To less dangerous waters.

He groaned theatrically. 'Dance lessons? Pottery? Good Lord.' Will tapped his finger against the table, his expression thoughtful. 'We could listen to live bands and definitely go skydiving—'

'Uh, *no!*'

'I could teach you to surf.'

'I'd consider that. Ice skating?'

'*Blergh*. Wet and cold. I'd consider pottery lessons if you'd consider dirt bike riding, getting out into the country. I know it's not a girl thing, but you might find it fun.'

Under the table Will's knee brushed Lu's and a bolt of awareness barrelled straight to his groin. Could he do this? Could he ignore this buzz of sexual attraction and be her friend?

Could he stop thinking about the kiss that never was? Stop replaying the way her eyes had half lowered and glinted green, the way her hands had held his hips, the brief taste of that perfect mouth?

He had to...there was no other choice. He was leaving soon and she was too dangerous to be around long-term because he suspected that she could—maybe—make him think about whether sparks could last and keep burning...

'Will? What do you think? Should we do this? *Can* we do this?'

He knew what she was asking... Could they do this without it getting complicated, messy? It was hard to meet her eyes, to see but ignore the corresponding flash of heat he recognised in them. He *had* to dismiss it, he realized. Just as she did. Because she wasn't ready to get involved he wouldn't get involved, so companionship was the only prize that was up for grabs.

'It'll be fine, Lu.'

If we can keep our hands off each other. Because if we can't then all bets are off.

Will sighed. He could really do with a stiff drink.

SIX

—

As they followed the signs past the main house to The Pottery Shed Lu flicked her finger against Will's shoulder. 'I thought I said that you should wear old clothes—not a nifty Zoo York T-shirt and cargo shorts.'

She was wearing an ancient shirt, cut-off jeans and flip-flops. Will looked down at his chest and sent her the evil eye. 'When I was packing my clothes in Auckland I didn't think I'd be going to pottery lessons! This is the oldest shirt I have here.'

'I could have lent you one of the twins' old T-shirts.' Lu said as they approached a barn at the back of the property. 'And stop moaning. I've agreed to go dirt bike riding next week.'

'I want to take you skydiving.'

'Not on your life.' Lu shuddered. 'And what do you mean...*take* me?'

'I'm certified to do tandem jumps...we could do one together.'

'Uh, let me think about that.' Lu pretended to peer

up at the sky. Two seconds later she spoke again. 'Thought about it...no. Nope. No way. Never.'

'Wuss,' Will said as a long, tall, elderly woman dressed in tie-dyed pants and a glowing caftan drifted from the barn.

Lu stepped forward and held out her hand. 'Hi, I'm Lu. Are you...?'

The woman's eyes drifted across their faces and she sent them a vague look. 'Kate. And I'm stoned.'

Lu looked at Will and lifted her eyebrows. 'You're *stoned*?'

'New supplier. His stuff is wicked good.'

'But our lesson...' Lu wailed, ignoring Will's smile of satisfaction.

Kate's hand wafted somewhere behind her head. 'Go on in—clay's in the bucket next to the wheel. Slap some on the wheel, hit the pedal, move your hands up and down. Make something. Lock up when you leave.'

'But... But...' Lu stuttered.

'*Namaste*,' Kate murmured, and weaved away in the general direction of the house.

Will folded his arms and watched her leave. 'Did you pay her?'

Lu pouted. 'No. I was going to pay her when we were finished.'

'Good. Then let's get out of here,' Will said, his expression a combination of smirky and relieved.

Lu narrowed her eyes at him. 'Uh-uh. You're not getting off that easily. Everything is set up...how hard can it be?'

Will groaned. 'Aw, Lu, come on! Let's go for a walk on the beach, have a beer, watch the sun go down.'

'Nope.' Lu said stubbornly. 'If I have to do dirt bikes then you have to try this.'

Will stepped through the open door to the studio, put his hands on his hips and looked around. Shelves packed with vases, bowls and vessels of every shape and form lined the room, and long tables covered with tools and boxes covered the back half of the shed. In the centre were three triangular-shaped desks with a potter's wheel on each and a bucket with what he presumed was clay next to each wheel.

Will pulled out a stool and sat down in front of one wheel, then looked from the desk to Lu. 'Um...what now?'

Lu's mouth twitched. 'I don't know. I haven't done this either...wait!' She reached across the table and picked up a plastic envelope. 'Instructions!'

Will leaned across and looked at the plastic enclosed paper. He shook his head and pointed to the heading. 'It's printed off the internet, Lu!'

'So?' Lu grinned. 'Let's try it.'

It seemed that he was about to try this thing. He knew that everything that could go wrong would. He didn't have an artistic bone in his body and he suspected that they were about to get dirty.

Really dirty. He looked around. 'Can you see any aprons?'

'Now who's being a wuss? We won't need any,' Lu told him. 'We'll be fine. So, first step... "Gather a small amount of clay—the size of two fists put together is plenty for someone just starting—and form it into a rough ball shape."'

Will dunked his hand in the bucket in front of him and lifted his eyebrows. Kind of the same texture as the mud he'd used to throw at his sisters.

'We need to knead it—get rid of the bubbles.'

'When do we get to play with the wheel thingy?' Will asked, trying to copy Lu's rather expert kneading technique. Which made him think of bread, which made him think of cake, and that reminded him...

'When am I getting my Austrian cake, by the way?'

'When I have time.' Lu peered down at the instructions. 'Maybe. So... "If you think all the air bubbles are out, shape it back into a rough ball."'

Will slapped the clay between his fingers.

'"Put the clay on the centre of the wheel head. The easiest way to do this is by throwing the clay with some force on the centre. Drip some water over it and spin the wheel fairly fast,"' she read.

'OK.' Will threw the clay down and hit the pedal of the wheel with some force. He watched his clay ball shoot across the wheel, skim the rim and fall on the floor. 'Whoops.'

Lu snorted with laughter.

'Think you can do better, Mermaid?'

What Lu didn't realise was that her pedal was next to his left foot . She was so busy trying to get it right that she didn't notice his foot sliding over hers until he pushed down hard. Her wheel spun furiously and her ball skidded across it. Lu yelped, turned in her seat and slipped her clay-covered hand onto his chest, leaving a perfect imprint of her fingers.

Blue-green eyes glinting with mirth met his as she

fought to find an innocent expression. 'It could have been worse,' she said on a shrug.

'It could?'

Lu grinned. 'I could've slapped your face.'

Will leaned forward and placed his wet, clay-covered hand on her cheek. 'What? Like this?'

Will kept his hand on her cheek as her mouth opened and closed like a guppy looking for air.

'You...you...'

He didn't think—couldn't think. He just placed his lips and swiped his mouth across hers in a kiss that was as shocking as it was stunning. Lu sighed into his mouth and planted her hands on his chest—intending, he was sure, to push him away. But her fingers curled into his T-shirt and gripped the fabric instead.

She tasted of sunshine and excitement, of cherry lip balm and surprise. Her perfume swirled up from her heated skin and he adored the scent. He yanked her off her stool and whirled her away from the wheel, up against a tall cupboard. He moved into her, needing to get closer, needing to feel her feminine form. Will lifted his hands to hold her face, tipping her head so that he could taste all of her mouth. Lu made a sound of approval that sent all his blood rushing south. She was heat and light, softness and courage, too much and not nearly enough. But he couldn't stop—didn't want to stop.

He knew he had to, because if he didn't he never would.

It took everything in him to lift his mouth from hers, to pull her head to his chest and rest his chin in her hair. 'God, Lu...'

Lu muttered something unintelligible and he thought he felt her lips flutter against his shirt.

'I wasn't going to do this,' he muttered, but the words were barely out of his mouth before he dropped it back to hers.

Her mouth parted to his insistent tongue and his hand drifted over her shirt, palmed her breast. Will felt another wicked flash of lust scuttle through him as she angled her head to allow him deeper access. Moving her hands, she ran her fingers across his taut stomach, let them drift lower before settling them low on his narrow hips.

'Lu, you're not helping!' Will pulled back, gripped her arms and kept her an arm's length away. He tried to inject some assertiveness into his voice. 'We aren't going to do this!'

Lu cocked her head at him. 'Do you always walk away?'

He knew what she meant. 'Yeah. Always.'

'Why?'

Will dragged his hand through his hair, pushing streaks of clay through it. 'Have you ever seen a fire when it's been put out?' he demanded. 'It's a wet, soggy, dirty, disgusting mess.'

'Ah, so you walk before it even gets the chance to become messy?'

Essentially. Some sparks, especially this one between him and Lu, had the potential to become a raging bush fire. But even bush fires couldn't rage for ever. And the bigger the fire, the bigger the mess. No, it was smarter just to keep this simple, platonic.

Because they had to work together, because he

really did have fun with her...but mostly because he hadn't been so tempted to walk into the blaze in a long, long time.

'OK, back up.' Lu wiggled her way out of his grip and leaned back against the cupboard. He looked at his hands. They were now only smeared with clay. She had clay in her hair. It was streaked over her shirt, her hips, down her neck.

'You're filthy,' she said, echoing his thoughts.

Will's finger drifted down her cheek. 'So are you. And, oh, crap...if we hadn't been going straight home we are now.'

Lu frowned. 'Why?'

Will motioned to her chest, where his palm print covered her left breast. 'Kind of a big clue about what we were up to.'

Lu looked down and closed her eyes. 'Pottery lesson a no-no, then?'

Will nodded, his expression rueful. 'It should definitely go on the things not to do list.'

'Along with skydiving,' Lu added quickly.

'Oh, I *will* get you up there.' Will promised.

After work on Friday Lu slipped into Old Joe's, a popular bistro in the middle of Florida Road. Pushing her sunglasses up onto her head, she smiled at Mak before placing her cheek on his and breathing in his scent. His pale pink shirt looked stunning against his skin, his tie was raspberry and his tailored pants were undoubtedly designer.

'I can't stay long. I'm meeting Will to go ten-pin bowling with him and some of the squad,' she told him, hanging her tote bag off a globe chair and sitting on the brightly coloured cushion.

'I don't have that much time either. I just wanted to tell you that Deon got into St Clares!'

Lu let out a delighted whoop before throwing her arms around Mak's neck and kissing his cheek.

'That's such fabulous news, Mak!'

'It is, but now that school is a reality the fear that he's going to be bullied again is back. In him and in me,' Mak admitted, sucking on what looked like a double-thick berry milkshake.

Lu fought temptation, lost, and ordered the chocolate equivalent. She was going for a run along the promenade later. She'd work it off then.

'He'll be fine, Mak. I promise. St Clare's doesn't tolerate any type of bullying.'

'I hope so,' Mak said eventually, leaning back in his chair. 'Anyway, back to you. Does this mean that you and Will are dating?'

Lu shook her head. 'No. Well...*no*.'

'That sounded convincing...not at all.' Mak pushed his empty glass away. 'So, what *is* going on between you?'

'I don't know... I think we're friends, but we have this sexual buzz.'

'So he's shoved his tongue down your throat?'

Lu gasped, blushed, and immediately thought back to that inferno-hot kiss they'd shared in the pottery studio. After holding her for a while he'd pulled back slightly, looked at her, and dived in again. His firm lips, the play of muscles under her hands, the feel of his big hand covering her not-so-big breast... His erection hard against her lower stomach, tenting his shorts...

He touched her and melted her brain. If he hadn't gathered up his car keys and mobile and yanked her to the car she would have let him take her there on that dusty floor.

Since then they'd both pretended it hadn't happened...and they were very, very careful to avoid touching each other.

'Can I get you anything else?'

Mak's eyes didn't leave Lu's face to look at the hovering waiter. 'A fire extinguisher would be helpful. I need to cool her down,' he said in a bone-dry voice.

'Makhosi!' Lu hissed. She blushed as she looked up at the confused waiter. 'Ignore him. Thanks, but we're fine.'

'So, do you want to answer my question now?'

'We kissed. So what? It's not a big deal...' It was *such* a big deal; she'd never had such an extreme reaction to being touched in her life. From nought to take-me-now in ten seconds flat. She heaved in some much needed air. 'I still can't and won't get involved with him, Mak.'

'And why not?'

'Because he is leaving in two months' time. Because he's not interested in anything but a casual friendship, having someone to hang out with.'

'So have a casual hook-up with him,' Mak suggested. 'It's not against the law, Lu.'

Lu closed her eyes. 'I can't, Mak.'

'Why? He's smart, good-looking and successful. Seems like a decent guy. I'm not seeing the problem.'

Lu shoved her fingers into her hair. 'He is strictly a

one-night stand kind of guy and I'm not a just-have-sex type of girl. And I work with him. And I have so much fun with him.'

Lu sipped and shrugged. 'After work I work on my photos, or I read, or I exercise. I think, plan. Try not to miss the twins. I need to—am *trying* to—get used to this new life without them, to being on my own. Then, when I feel the walls closing in on me, I call Will and we go out and have an absolute blast. We laugh, Mak—hard. Often. We talk or don't talk...there's no pressure and I like that.' Lu stared at the huge African mask dominating the opposite wall. 'Sure, I'd like sex, but not if it means sacrificing the fun we're having.'

Mak leaned forward and touched her hand. 'Just be careful, Lu. I don't want to mop up your tears, hon.'

'You won't have to, Mak.'

Casual linen three-quarter pants, a funky brown and gold T-shirt, beaded sandals and new jewellery. Will took in Lu's outfit as she moved across the staff dining room towards the table where he sat with the older members of the team. OK, different...he thought.

His gaze travelled up her throat. He remembered that the spot between her ear and her jaw was very tender, and that she'd vibrated in his arms when he'd nibbled her just there. Kissing her had been a mistake, he thought, not for the first time. His pants grew substantially smaller. Mostly because all he thought about was doing it again.

Her mouth had been hot and demanding—and, talking about her mouth...good God. What on earth had she stained her lips with? Mulberries? Will leaned back and looked at her properly: too much blusher, smoky eyes, a bottle of mascara. She looked glossy, but she also looked like every other girl he'd ever dated.

Slick, superficial, sophisticated...*hard*.

He heard the low wolf whistles and the compliments of his two lunch companions: Jabu, the Rays' captain, and Matt Johnson, whom he knew had the hots for Lu. Would he have to have a chat with Matt about keeping his distance from Lu? Maybe.

Matt needed to know that Lu was *way* off-limits.

Will looked at Lu and wished he could pull her off to the showers and wash that make-up off her. He wanted his Lu back: clean skin—her freckles were all but hidden now—clear eyes...normal. He wanted her make-up-free, naturally...*normal*.

Crap.

When a guy started thinking that natural was gorgeously normal he was neck deep in the brown stuff... or about to fall into the brown stuff. Neither scenario was vaguely attractive.

Lu slid down into the empty chair opposite him and reached for the salt to shake over her chicken salad.

'New look, Lu?' Matt asked.

'Experimenting.'

Lu batted her eyelashes at him and Will felt his stomach contract.

'What do you think?'

'Hot,' Matt answered.

He ran his finger over the tattoo of a naughty angel on her shoulder. Will considered breaking his fingers.

'Cool tat.'

What the hell...? She'd got a tattoo? Not that it had

anything to do with him...except he didn't like the idea of ink on that amazing, smooth, clear expanse of skin. Skin he'd all too briefly explored, discovered, wanted to taste again.

Matt tipped his head back to look at her shoulder again. 'Ah, it's just a henna tat—it'll be gone in six weeks.'

'Thank the Lord,' Will muttered under his breath. He ignored Lu's quizzical look, took a healthy sip from his glass of water and pushed his empty plate away. He stretched out his leg and the inside of his calf brushed her bare foot. He felt the bolt of lust shoot up to his groin.

He raised reluctant eyes and saw his desire reflected in hers—along with a solid dose of irritation. She wanted him but didn't want to want him. She wanted him to compliment her on her new look but didn't want him to know that she cared. Will ran his hand along his jaw. This was getting a bit too complicated, a little more intense than he'd bargained for.

And he *still* wanted to take the make-up off her face. Take her back to natural Lu.

'Would you mind signing these for me? I'd be so grateful.' Lu was handing out letter-size photos and dishing out black felt-tipped markers.

'What's going on?' he asked as he took his own photograph and a pen.

Lu rested her forearms on the table. 'You remember that I mentioned Mak has a highly functioning, Down Syndrome son? He's rugby-obsessed and thinks that I am the luckiest girl in the world to know you guys. You're his favourite player, Jabu.'

Jabu's face split into a huge smile. 'Cool.'

Lu wiped her mouth with a paper serviette and Will was grateful to see a lot of the mulberry stain disappear. Three more layers and that gorgeous mouth would be back. 'I've looked after Deon a lot over the years. He's a nice kid. But he's physically small for his age and he's terrified about starting a new school. He was badly bullied at his last school. He's about to start at St Clare's—'

'But that's a mainstream school, not a special needs school,' Matt interrupted. 'I went there; they don't have special needs kids.'

'They introduced a new programme about five years back to integrate kids with special needs into the mainstream school. It's a huge success. I also know the school well. My brothers attended it. Mak is a bundle of nerves for Deon. He's trying to be brave but is scared witless...anyway, I said I'd go with them on his first day.'

'Which is...?' Will asked.

'Tomorrow.' Lu forked up some chicken and waved her fork at the pack of photos. 'I thought that if Deon ran into any bullying he could offer up some signed photos from his Rays heroes to talk his way out of it.'

Will dashed his signature across a photograph and smiled. 'No problem.'

Lu pulled to a stop outside St Clare's and turned in her seat to look backwards. Deon was looking a little grey, his hands were trembling, and his knee bounced up and down. Mak was looking equally nauseous. He might be tough and forthright, but he was a marshmallow when it came to his son.

Lu touched his shoulder before leaning back to pat Deon on the thigh. 'I told you that my brothers went here and that it's a really nice school? Remember that Mr Klimt, the principal, doesn't tolerate bullying.'

'Mr Klimt doesn't go into the boys' bathrooms,' Deon said in his slow, measured voice.

Lu sighed. The child might be challenged but he was not a fool. How was she going to get either of them out of the car and up the steps that led into the school? They were both anxiously watching the streams of laughing, smiling chatty kids mingling on the grass, within the school quad, leaning against walls and doors.

They looked confident and happy...no wonder Deon and Mak were terrified. Even she was feeling a bit intimidated.

'I want to go home,' Deon said, and dropped his chin to his neck.

She couldn't cry. That wouldn't help anyone! Terrified or not, someone had to take charge. 'Right, let's get your stuff together, dude.'

Lu sighed as her mobile rang. She picked it up and sighed at the display. 'It's really not a good time, Will.'

'It's a very good time,.' Will replied, laughter in his voice. 'Tell the kid that his posse has arrived.'

'What?'

'Look in your review mirror, Mermaid.'

Lu slid a glance to her mirror and laughter bubbled up in her throat. Walking down the pavement, dressed in their Rays training uniforms, looking as intimidating as all hell, were Jabu, Matt and three other prominent Rays players. Will and Kelby walked behind them. Will had his mobile in his hand.

Lu swallowed down her emotion and turned to Deon, her face alight with excitement. 'OK, Deon, this is a mega big day for you.' She winked at Mak, who'd just caught sight of the players now coming to a stop outside her car. His jaw fell to his lap. Lu reached over and lifted Deon's chin. 'I know this is scary, but some special people thought that you might need someone to see you into school. Say hello to my friend Jabu.'

Jabu ducked his head inside the car and as long as she lived Lu knew she would never forget the look on the little boy's face when he saw his biggest sporting hero. The back door flew open and Deon tumbled into Jabu's enormous arms. Jabu held him with ease and calmly ignored his shaking as he introduced him to the rest of his team mates.

Lu looked at Mak, whose Adam's apple was bobbing with restrained emotion. 'Did you know about this?' he demanded.

Lu shook her head and sniffed. 'Not a damn thing. Will must have organised it.'

Mak pressed the heels of his hands against his eyes. 'I'm really liking this guy, Lu.'

Will looked at the commotion they were causing and grinned. He'd forgotten the enthusiasm kids could display—that wide eyed excitement. He'd felt exactly the same when he'd met his sporting heroes as a kid.

Then Will looked at Lu's face as she climbed out of her car and grinned at the emotions crossing it.

Wonder, amazement, joy. Yeah, this was *so* worth organising.

Kelby jammed him in the ribs. 'Take that goofy look off your face, Scott. You look like a sap.'

'I don't do goofy,' Will said through gritted teeth.

'Well, you sure as hell are doing *something*!' Kelby grinned as they stood a little way off from the rest of the team. 'So what prompted this, mate? I mean, I'm not complaining...' he gestured to a couple of sports photographers who were walking across the road towards them '...it's great publicity. But it's way out of your scope as caretaker coach.'

'Uh...' Will tugged at the collar of his shirt.

'Could it have anything to do with the fact that you are doing my press photographer, who obviously has a very special relationship with this kid?'

Will shuffled on his feet. 'I'm not sleeping with her; we're just friends, Kelby.'

Kelby roared with laughter and slapped Will on the back. 'Yeah, right! You've never done anything like this before.'

Will gritted his teeth. 'Kelby, we're friends...like you suggested. That's it.'

Kelby's laughter faded, surprise dominated and he shook his head. 'Oh, my poor, confused young friend!' He grinned again and slapped Will between his shoulderblades. Again. 'You, dude, are ass-deep in woman trouble. I *love* it!'

Will was thinking about punching him when he felt Lu's approach. He looked around when a small hand rested on his bicep.

'You arranged this, didn't you?' Lu asked, tears in her eyes.

God, he did one nice thing and everyone got soppy!

'Jabu and I had a chat about it. He was bullied at school so he knows what it's like. The Rays also promote anti-bullying on their website,' Will replied.

'Thank you. I'm overwhelmed.'

'No worries. It was easy enough to do,' Will said. He caught Mak's eye and shook his hand, brushed off his gratitude.

It seemed as if a good portion of the school's pupils were gathered around them when Jabu raised his hand and the crowd quietened. 'OK—any rugby boys here?'

Hands shot up into the air. 'Who is your favourite team?'

'Rays! Rays! Rays!'

The Rays players smiled and after a minute Jabu lifted his hand again. 'This is Deon. He's a new boy here today and he's our number one fan. We need our fans' support, and sometimes our fans need our support. Deon needs our support today because it's not easy walking into a new school. So, while we might not be here every minute of every day, we're going to be looking out for him. And for when we're not here we're appointing our own boys to make sure he finds his way around OK.'

Jabu bent down and had a quick discussion with Deon.

'Eleven-year-old rugby players, step forward!' he bellowed, and a number of boys belted out of the crowd to stand eagerly in front of Jabu and the rest of the huge players. 'You show Deon the ropes and we'll arrange that your team gets to train with us, at our field, once a month for the next three months. Deal?'

'Deal!' The piping voices bounced back.

Lu lifted her hand to her heart and looked up at Will with shining eyes. 'You'd do that?'

'Apparently Kelby's been asking Carter to do it as part of a community service programme but he wasn't prepared to consider it. Old school. The other clubs do it with different schools all the time.' Will shrugged. 'It's for an hour. It's nothing.'

'It's everything to the kids,' Lu said as the bell rang.

But the children didn't move. They were too busy jostling for the players' attention and demanding autographs.

Will grinned when he saw two boys, obviously St Clare rugby players, standing on either side of Deon to protect him from the crowd. 'I think our work here is done.'

A shrill whistle broke their eye contact and kids and adults all froze as a short, round man bustled down the steps, his face red with what Lu knew was fake annoyance.

'What is going on here? Why aren't you in class?' Mr Klimt roared, but Will saw his face soften as her eyes swept over Deon and his new bodyguards. He placed his hands on his hips. 'What are these big men doing here? Who are they?' he demanded, faking displeasure.

A collective groan rose from the crowd. One brave soul eventually dared to answer him. 'Mr Klimt, they are Rays players! Jabu and Matt.'

'Really? I thought they were ballerinas! Mr Johnson? Is that you?' The crowd fell silent as short Mr Klimt looked up—and up—into Matt's face.

'Yes, sir.' Matt over-exaggerated his grimace and some of the kids snorted with suppressed laughter.

'And what are you doing on Friday afternoon, Mr Johnson?' The principal demanded.

'I don't believe I'm doing anything, Mr Klimt...sir.'

'Good. If I am not mistaken, I believe you still owe me two hours of detention.'

SEVEN

———

Later that afternoon Lu was in the players' lounge, working on her laptop, when she heard low, masculine laughter and Will, Jabu, Matt and Kelby walked in. Everyone but the suited Kelby was now dressed in casual clothes, their hair wet from the shower.

Lu was getting to know their weekly schedule; it was Wednesday, so that meant that after they'd returned to the stadium from St Clare's they'd spent the morning watching a video analysis of their opposition for the weekend's game and then they'd hit the field. Full-contact rugby and Will had been in the thick of it.

She could see a scrape on his knee and a bruise forming above his elbow. He did not believe in shouting instructions from the sideline. He put his body on the line practice after practice. And, judging by the satisfaction she could see in his eyes, he loved it. Despite their deal to keep it friendly, he made her heart go flippity-flop every time he sent her that engaging grin, and with the way his eyes heated when they settled on her face. Lu closed her laptop lid as he took the seat opposite her and offered her a taste of his just-opened soda.

Lu took a sip and handed it back. 'You look like you took a couple of hits on the field.'

Will rubbed his shoulder. 'I did. Jabu is the human equivalent of a Sherman tank.'

'Thanks for what you did this morning. Again.'

'No problem. Again,' Will answered as the others sat down around them.

Lu greeted them and asked what their plans were for the evening.

Jabu yawned. 'Nothing more exciting than an early night. Training was brutal this afternoon; Wednesdays are the worst day.'

Will grinned. 'Whiner.'

Jabu lifted a lazy middle finger and yawned again. Looking over Lu's head to the television mounted on the wall, he sat up and reached for the remote control on the table in front of him. 'Hey, Will—your ex is on.'

Unlike the others, who immediately looked at the screen, Lu looked at Will. His face tightened instinctively, his lips thinned and his eyes darkened. Jabu adjusted the volume control and Lu reluctantly looked over her shoulder.

Beautiful. Lean and long, finely muscled. Long blonde hair, big blue eyes, legs that went on for ever. High cheekbones and a quirky mouth completed the package. How and why had Will let her go?

'Do you mind if we watch it, Will?' Matt demanded. 'Your ex is a fox!'

'Knock yourself out,' Will replied, looking for all the

world as if he didn't give a damn. Which he *so* did. She could see it in his flattened mouth, in his tapping finger on the side of his thigh.

They listened to Jo talking about her training schedule, her fitness regime. Lu cast the occasional look at Will and sighed every time. His face was a mask of control, his body seemingly relaxed but his eyes radiating tension and frustration.

The interviewer was asking another question. 'So, Jo, you're now ranked at number two in the world, but there was a time when your off-court antics garnered a lot of news.'

Lu saw the flash of panic in Will's eyes but still he didn't react.

'Yeah, it's not a time in my life I'm proud of...'

'Shortly after your divorce you turned your life around. You embraced religion, cleaned up your act. Why do you think it took Will Scott so much longer to do the same thing?'

Everyone else in the room inhaled and Will forced out a laugh. 'Because I was having too much damn fun, jackass.'

His friends laughed, relieved when they heard his jokey tone. Only Kelby, Lu thought, might suspect that he was acting his socks off.

'It was only two years—and I wouldn't presume to talk on Will's behalf,' Jo replied.

'Your marriage was characterised by fighting and making up. When you were happy you were ecstatic—when you were fighting it was obvious. Despite that, the world thought your marriage would survive. So what precipitated your divorce?'

'God, why do people still *care*?' Will demanded. 'Aren't there any twenty-year-olds behaving badly these days?'

'Not as many as we'd like.' Matt shook his head sadly. 'And few of them are as good entertainment as you and Jo were. You two *rocked*!'

'Until I nearly lost my career because I couldn't come to work sober or at the very least not hungover,' Will said, speaking over Jo's reply. 'And talking of that... while I've got the CEO, the Captain and the Vice-Captain here all at the same time, with no other ears listening, you guys need to do something about Campher. He's on something. Drugs, booze, pills, steroids—I don't know what, but it's something.'

Jabu swore. 'It hasn't popped up in the drug tests.'

'I'm telling you he's on something,' Will said. 'I'm only here for another eight weeks. You still have the rest of the season with him. I'll order a comprehensive drug screening, but I wanted to run it past you first.'

Three heads nodded their agreement and then turned back to the television screen.

'Are you proud of what he's done? Achieved?'

The interviewer was still talking about Will.

'Sure. I always knew that Will was destined for great things. We both just took a detour, lost our way for a bit. Why are people still wanting to hear about it?'

'You were good entertainment value. So, let's talk about your sponsorship deals, Jo.'

Matt jabbed his finger upwards. 'You see—he agrees with me! Now you're just old and boring, Scott.'

Will stood up and swatted Matt across the head. 'Funny—you didn't say that when I face-planted you this afternoon. I need to do some paperwork before I leave, so I'm going to head off.'

He hadn't even made eye contact with her, Lu thought as she watched his departing back. Yep, he was good at concealing his emotions—but so was she, and she knew what to look for.

Will had instinctively headed for the far corner of the gym, avoided the fancy equipment and yanked a pair of gloves from the shelf on the far wall. Jamming them between his knees, he pulled off his T-shirt, divested himself of his trainers and socks and left the pile of clothes on the floor next to an exercise mat. Pulling the gloves on, he proceeded to punch and kick the stuffing out of the dangling bag.

Kelby had made him do this years ago. Every time he'd felt out of control and frustrated he'd found a bag and pummelled it. At one time he'd been spending so much time with the punch bag that he signed up for Thai kick-boxing and learnt to do it properly.

He only ever did this now when he was feeling particularly stressed or when...*punch, kick, punch*...he felt out of control.

What was it about watching Jo this evening that had pushed every button he had? She was a prominent personality but he'd learnt how to hear about her, see her on the screen, read about her, with a detachment that came from a decade apart. Why now?

It had nothing to do with Jo, he realised, and everything to do with the life he'd led when he was with her—the person he'd been. Fun, crazy, spontaneous... out of control.

Being with Lu, spending time with her, reminded him of that person he'd once been. Oh, there was no alcohol or drugs involved this time, no dancing on bars and wrecking cars, but like during the best times he'd had back then they *did* have fun. They laughed. They talked.

They *didn't* screw like bunnies.

And they were rapidly becoming friends—proper friends. Instead of just finding her to be a fun person to hang with he was finding that he wanted to tell her things, open up. And that scared him to death. Sex would have been so much easier. This? Not so much.

Being with Lu made him feel like the best version of who he'd been as a young man. Fun. Spontaneous. Curious.

Alive.

He'd been all of that and more. He'd been touted as the most promising young player in a generation—a team man, an amazing talent. Then he'd met Jo and had—oh, so willingly—fallen into the wild life she'd embraced. They'd married on a whim in Bali, and their life together had been fuelled by booze and dope and causing as much chaos as they could. They'd been untouchable, arrogant and superior. He'd started to work less and believe his own press more, had become enamoured of the adulation and adoration of fans and groupies. For a long time he'd thought he was a special person with a talent for rugby. It had taken Kelby to make him realise that he was just an ordinary guy with a special talent for the game.

As for their marriage...he'd been bored with her within three months and hadn't been able to understand why. Sure, she was smoking hot—but she was also bright. Something he'd frequently forgotten. She could be hysterically funny, had superior mattress skills and a personality as big as the sun. There had been no reason to get bored with her. She was everything he'd ever thought he'd wanted but...

The spark had died. Quickly.

Could he be blamed for having doubts about his ability to stay in a relationship, to commit to a relationship? He'd been handed everything any guy anywhere in the world would sell his soul for and he hadn't wanted it. But he'd kept it going—and he suspected she had too—because he'd earned big bragging points for being married to the sexiest woman in the world. And he'd liked the attention.

He hadn't had the balls to break it off...until she did. Apparently there really *wasn't* any good excuse for having an Argentinean woman in your room at three in the morning when you were married.

Will snapped a full round-house kick at the punching bag and followed the kick with an upper-cut when the bag came roaring back towards him. He'd been a yellow-bellied coward and after the divorce, instead of putting up his hand and saying sorry, he had bounced from affair to affair, party to party, bottle to bottle, making more of an ass of himself every month, losing a little more respect for himself every day.

If it hadn't been for Kelby...

Will glanced at his watch. He'd been at it for a half-hour and he hadn't even noticed. Sweat snaked down his bare spine into the back of his shorts and his hair was matted to his head. Using the back of his wrist, he pushed the hair back from his face and hauled air into his lungs. The adrenalin and anger were gone and he realised that he was utterly exhausted, his muscles beyond fatigued. Between the run this morning, the full body contact practice this afternoon and beating the crap out of this bag, he was skating on the edge of physical exhaustion.

Will grabbed the sides of the bag and rested his sticky forehead on the thick plastic. Well, he should sleep well tonight—that was if he didn't start thinking about his crappy past. And Lu. And how much longer he could keep his hands off her...

Will turned on hearing the gentle slap of Lu's sandals as she crossed the gym.

'How long have you been here?' he demanded, pulling off one glove with his teeth, then ridding himself of the other.

Lu tossed him a bottle of water which he caught with his free hand. 'A while. Want to talk about it?'

Will cracked the lid and took a long sip before sinking to sit on an exercise mat. He held Lu's sympathetic eyes as water slid down his throat.

'Nothing to talk about,' he said when he'd lowered the bottle.

Lu tipped her head and shook her head. 'The past loses its power when it's talked about. Secrets too.'

'What would you know about secrets and the power they hold over people, Lu?'

Lu's eyes sharpened and hardened. 'Try clearing out your parents' personal effects on your own at nineteen and say that again, Scott.'

Will winced. '*Ouch*. Did you learn some stuff you'd rather not know?'

Lu folded her arms and tapped her foot. 'Yes. So don't try and take the high road with me about secrets. I know what I'm talking about.'

Will stretched out his legs and placed his hands on the mat behind him. 'Bet you haven't shared them with your brothers.'

Lu twisted her lips. 'There are some things they don't need to know.'

'And there are some things the world doesn't need to know about *my* life.'

Lu's mouth thinned. 'I'm not talking about the world, Will. I'm suggesting that you talk things through so that you don't have to kick a bag.'

'I like kicking the bag.'

Lu threw up her hands. 'OK, if you're going to be facetious then I give up. I'll just go and leave you to it.'

The words were stiff and staccato and Will sighed at the hurt look that passed over her face. A part of him wished he could tell her, wished he *could* trust enough to talk it over with her, to confess his stupidity. But apart from the fact that he was not in the habit of talking about himself he thought that talking to Lu about it would be akin to slicing himself open and watching himself bleed. He also didn't want to see the look of disgust on her face, to see her disappointment in the man he'd used to be...a man he suspected still lurked under his tightly held cloak of control.

'I'll see you when I see you.'

Lu turned to go but Will's leg shot out, gently catching Lu behind the knees. She tumbled to the mat, landing on her back next to him.

'What the—?'

Before she could say another word Will rolled onto her and covered her mouth with his. Her fist clenched against his shoulder, but as his tongue touched hers her tension disappeared and her hand opened, fingers splaying over him and branding his bare skin.

Will pulled his head back to look down at her, raised his hand so that the tips of his fingers brushed her cheek.

'Lu, if there was anybody I could tell it would be you. I just don't...can't...talk about it.'

She echoed his action, lifting her hand to touch his face. 'You need to talk to somebody about it. You can't kick the hell out of a bag every time you get angry.'

'Actually, I can.' Will's eyes glinted down at her. 'I need to. It's the only way to relieve the tension.'

He knew that Lu felt his erection along her hipbone—could feel his accelerated heartbeat beneath her hand. They both knew it but didn't acknowledge the other, tried and tested way to relieve stress. He liked feeling her under him, but he also liked the fact that she'd noticed that he was out of sorts, that she cared enough to make the effort to comfort him.

Will's eyes collided with hers and underneath the attraction he saw sympathy there, and understanding. Flat-out affection. He could care for this woman. He really could. But when it all went south and the flames died—as they always did—he suspected that he'd be left with third degree burns.

Not an option.

Will reluctantly rolled off her and heard Lu's sweet sigh of exasperation. He knew how she felt. He craved her too. They lay on their backs on the mat for a while, staring at the ceiling.

Lu rolled her head on the mat to look at the bag and couldn't believe she was about to say what she was about to say.

'Does it work for sexual tension too?'

Will sighed. 'Not as good as a cold shower but... yeah.'

'Want to teach me?'

'Are you sexually frustrated, Mermaid?'

Will's hand slid over hers and squeezed. She knew that he'd been aiming for a jokey tone, but his words had come out pained instead.

And instead of sounding cool and sophisticated *her* words were soft and sad. 'Well, I have this guy that I'm mega-attracted to, and in a fit of madness we agreed that it would be better to just be friends. I'm having the best fun with him, but sometimes I just want to...'

Will pulled in a hot breath. 'Nail him?'

'Yeah.' Lu wrinkled her nose as her rueful eyes met his. Like him, she'd been aiming to lighten the tension, but instead she'd just tumbled them into a miasma of emotion. Lu wanted to look away and couldn't— wanted to make a sassy comment but couldn't find any words to say.

Will's hand contracted around hers. 'God, Lu, I know how you feel.'

'I'm having so much fun with you and I don't want to spoil it, so I'll punch a bag if that helps,' Lu gabbled.

Will rolled to his side and placed his free hand on

her face. 'I don't want to spoil it, either so I'll teach you to box,' he said, his voice rough. 'But if we don't get up soon we won't need to punch anything.'

Lu turned her face into his hand and dropped a kiss on his palm. 'OK.'

But they still lay there for a while longer, his one hand holding hers, the other on her face, feeling physically and emotionally connected.

Whoops, Lu thought. That wasn't supposed to happen.

It was late Sunday afternoon and Lu was attempting, unsuccessfully, to make the transition from lying on her surfboard to standing up. Will, standing hip-deep in the Indian Ocean off North Beach, was trying to hide his smile.

'Stop laughing at me, you jerk!' Lu shouted at him as she popped up from under a two-foot wave. 'We weren't all born super co-ordinated!'

'You'll get there,' Will told her, laughing as she rubbed her face.

She would have given up hours ago, but she knew that learning to surf was a way to get some distance from their emotionally charged discussion in the gym the other night.

Constantly looking like an idiot and getting sand in her bikini bottoms was a small price to pay to put the fun and laughter back into their...whatever it was they had.

'I would like to point out, for the record, that we only seem to be doing things *you* like to do.' Lu slapped her hands on her hips. 'We never made it to that art exhibition—and what happened to dance classes?'

'We're going to the photography exhibition,' Will pointed out.

'That's in two weeks' time,' Lu retorted. 'I'm sick of sucking at sport.'

Will laughed. 'Say that again—five times and fast.'

'I'm sip at supping at...*aaargh*!'

Will laughed as he walked through the water to her and took her board from her grasp. 'That's enough for today; Mak and Deon look ready to leave anyway.'

Lu looked towards the beach, where Mak and Deon stood at the water's edge, Deon's head droopy against Mak's arms. The four of them had spent the afternoon there and Will and Mak had spent hours tossing a rugby ball to Deon, much to his delight. They'd all taken turns to swim with him too, and the little guy was utterly, happily exhausted.

Lu scooped him up, gave him a huge kiss and handed him over to Will, who piggy-backed him back to their bags and towels scattered over the still hot sand. Will put Deon on his feet, helped Mak load up their bags and rubbed Deon's head.

'Are you coming to the stadium with the St Clare's kids on Tuesday?'

Deon nodded. 'I'm their main man.'

Will grinned. 'That you are. Later, dude.'

'Later, dude,' Deon echoed and the adults laughed.

After they'd left, Will cocked his head at Lu. 'I'm going back in. You coming?'

Lu nodded and they turned back to the sea, sighing as the warm Indian Ocean crept higher the further in they went.

'School and work day tomorrow,' Lu said, as the waves lapped against her chest.

She wondered what the twins had been up to today...if they'd had as much fun as she had. On days like these—beach days, happy days—she missed them with every cell in her body. She'd been fighting the urge to call them all day, and the couple of messages she'd sent them still, as of ten minutes ago, remained unread. They were never without their phones, so what had they been *doing* all day?

Lu felt Will's thumb brush the space between her eyebrows and she turned her head to look at him. 'Sometimes you drift away and then this frown appears.'

'Sun in my eyes,' Lu replied blithely.

'Yeah, tell me another one.' Will snorted.

Lu snuck a look at his frustrated face. 'How come you want me to talk but you don't...or won't?'

'Because I'm a guy.'

Lu's snort was bigger than his. 'We're really good at having fun and really bad at talking to each other about the things that go deep,' she commented. 'I know that you were seriously upset after seeing your ex on TV—'

'I wasn't.'

'Will.' Just her saying his name had his protest dying on his lips. 'And I'm missing the twins. Yet we still try to pretend that everything is fine.'

'I don't know how to—' Will stopped and automatically reached out to steady her as a large wave broke over them. Using his strength, he planted his feet and kept her upright as water rushed over her head. Lu linked her arms around his neck, droplets of water on her face.

'I wish you'd talk to me, Will,' Lu murmured, frustrated. He was holding back, keeping her at arm's length mentally, and she didn't like it. If he could push *her* out of her comfort zone why couldn't she do the same for him?

The problem was that he just had to look at her with those hot eyes and she forgot about comfort zones and talking and anything else but her need to have his mouth on hers.

Will kissed her shoulder as he whispered, 'I'll tell you that I think you are incredibly beautiful."

Lu hiccupped a laugh. 'Freckly and skinny.'

'Beautifully, gorgeously freckly and skinny,' Will insisted. He looked down into her eyes. 'I don't know how to do this...the other stuff...the talking stuff. I can't do it—haven't the skills. But this...this I know.'

Yes, Lu thought. And it was the perfect end to a wonderful day as Will's tongue slipped into her mouth and his hands pulled her hips into his.

Her stomach pressed against his erection and her breasts were flattened against his chest. She felt uninhibited and free. His actions under the water were hidden from the last few people on the beach, and the surfers were too far away for them to see and too uninterested to give a hoot. Scooting her hand up his hip, she caressed his stomach, feeling the wonder of the warm skin over hard muscles. Will responded by cupping her breast, instinctively seeking her nipple, which instantly bloomed in his hand.

Lu gasped and wrenched her mouth away from his, arching her back as she buried her face in his neck and swiped her tongue across his skin. This was what she'd been missing—this intensity, this flood of lust and emotion that she hadn't experienced with a man in a long, long time.

Will groaned as he snuck his hands under her pink bikini top and tangled her tongue with his. He sensed her frustration and responded with a silent chuckle. She wasn't the only one who craved more. But suddenly this wasn't about him. This was about Lu and the pleasure he could give her—the pleasure he knew she hadn't experienced in a long, long time...if ever.

'Wrap your legs around my waist, honey,' he murmured against her mouth.

Lu, eyes glazed with passion, obliged. Will dropped his gaze to look down between them. Her thighs were slim and baby-smooth; he could feel her hipbone under the palm of his other hand. A beaded ring was hooked through her belly button.

'Just enjoy, Lu,' Will told her, and saw the soft reply in her eyes, tasted it in her lifted lips.

She became compliant beneath him, her trust that he would take care of her blindingly obvious. Will braced himself by pushing his feet into the sand while kissing her—he couldn't get enough of her luscious mouth. He moved his hand over her ankle and calf, tracing his way up her thigh, lingering to knead her bottom. His long fingers slid under her bikini bottom to stroke lightly between her legs. He ignored her whimper and felt her intake of breath as he moved his hand between them and trailed it over her, bending his head to kiss her again, feeling her throb beneath his fingertips. His fingers—urgent now—slid into her furrows, automatically finding her nub, causing her to lift her hips, thrusting into his hand. Astounded at her passionate reaction, by the tension he could feel in her, Will felt immensely powerful, intensely male.

He felt her orgasm against his hand, saw it in her eyes, heard it in her whimpered cries.

She made him feel more of a man...

Long, long minutes later she dropped her feet back into the sand and pushed her hands through her hair. As long as he lived Will knew that he'd never forget Lu standing chest deep in the sea, tipping her face up to catch the last of the sunshine, looking a lot like the mermaid he sometimes imagined her to be.

'What are we going to do about this, Lu?' he demanded as they walked back towards the beach. 'We're dancing around it and something is going to have to give—soon.'

Lu ran her hands through her hair again, making spikes. 'I don't know, Will! I *don't*! I know that I want you, but I don't want to stop having fun with you either—and that was the deal, remember? Sex and you walk. No sex and you don't.'

'Whose stupid idea was that?' he muttered under his breath. 'Oh, that must have been yours, Scott. Moron.'

It *was* the deal, and he'd thought it made sense all those weeks back, when his life had made sense. Will grabbed a towel off the beach mat and swiped it across his face. He didn't know how much longer he could re-sist her—resist the temptation to take her to bed, to make her his. But she terrified him. She had the abil-ity to make him lose focus, to do the things, *feel* the things he'd used to when his life had been out of con-trol. Like acting first and thinking later. His life had the potential to spiral out of control when he allowed that side of his personality to rule.

With Lu, his devil-may-care side was demanding a lot more decision making opportunities and—what had Kelby called him?—Mr Disciplined Control was taking a beating.

Either way, he felt as if he was fighting a demonic alien invasion with a water pistol in a desert.

Lu could see all her confusion reflected in Will's eyes. He wanted her—she'd have to be dead not to re-alise that—but he didn't *want* to want her. As for her, she knew that if they moved from friends to lovers then she would be inviting a whole bunch of compli-cated craziness into her life. It would be a lot harder to say goodbye to a lover than a friend when he left, and even worse it would be so much more difficult to keep her mind thinking *friends*, her body think-ing *lover* and her heart out of the equation if she was sleeping with him.

Lu held his gaze, hating his rigid self-control. He wasn't going to ask her to bed, wasn't going to take that step. If only they could really talk to each other…

What would she say?

I love spending time with you, she told him silently. *But I don't think that I'm ready for a relationship, strings or not. I'm just getting to know myself again, learning to*

*be on my own. I'm finally coming into myself, learning who
I am without the responsibility of raising the twins. If we
hook up I'll have someone back in my life and I don't know
if I'm ready for that. Because you are a strong character,
a protector, another alpha personality, and when you go
I'll be back to square one, learning to be on my own again.*

It was so hard to resist him, and it would be easy
to let him slide into all the empty spaces in her heart
and home that the boys had left. But for the first time
in her life she had to think about what was best for
her and, as much as she thought it would be fun, she
didn't think it was a smart move long-term. For the
first time in a decade she didn't have to worry about
someone else—and she liked it.

Lu sighed. 'Will?'

'Yeah?'

'Do you know that neither of us has said anything
for ten minutes?'

Will shrugged. 'OK...so?'

'If we need to think about it so much maybe we
should leave things the way they are?'

Will twisted his lips. 'Confused and horny?'

Give the man another gold star, Lu thought morosely.

EIGHT

'So, Carter has been cleared to come back to work in a month...'

Will stared at Kelby, nonplussed. 'That means that I can leave Durban in a month or so?'

'We'll pay you out for the full three months.'

He didn't give a toss about the money. It was leaving Lu earlier than he'd bargained for that was threatening to throw him into a tailspin.

'Also, at the director's meeting last night, the board agreed that Carter will retire in six months. I can offer you a position as consultant coach until then and a five-year contract as head coach when he's gone. What do you think?'

Will yanked his thoughts away from Lu. 'Giving control back to Carter sucks. I don't know if I can do it and then work under him.'

'It's for six months, dude! And he's a good coach. You'd learn a lot from him.'

Will placed his hands on Kelby's desk and straightened his arms, thinking it through. 'I've been getting other offers from other teams. Firm consultant and then head coach offers from Melbourne and Auckland.'

Kelby leaned back in his chair. 'Have you talked to Lu about any of this?'

Will frowned at him. 'No.'

'Don't you think you should?'

Will stood up and folded his arms belligerently. Because he was still reeling at the thought of how much he didn't want to leave her, he narrowed his eyes at Kelby's comment. 'She isn't a factor. We're just friends.'

'Friends! Yeah, keep telling yourself that.' Kelby shook his head in disbelief. 'And if you let her go then you're crazier than I gave you credit for.'

Let her go? He hadn't even *had* her yet! He'd spent most of last night tossing and turning, and when he *had* slept his dreams had been super-hot and had involved him taking Lu fifty ways to Sunday.

As a result he was tired, irritable, and still as confused and even hornier than he had been yesterday afternoon. He thought he was either a saint or an idiot to have dropped her off at home after their day on the beach and left her there.

No, he was definitely an idiot.

Will glanced at his watch. 'I've got to go. I'm late as it is.'

Kelby frowned. 'Late for what?'

'Game analysis. It's at four.'

'Do you *ever* read any of the memos I send you? I asked for game analysis to be postponed because Lu is doing that nude calendar shoot with the squad this evening.'

Will turned around very slowly and sent Kelby his death-ray glare. 'What. Did. You. Say?'

Kelby didn't do a very good job of trying to hide his smile. 'Twelve of the franchise clubs are collaborating on a calendar featuring the various teams to raise money for charity. Each franchise is responsible for capturing their own discreet image of the team.'

'And Lu is doing this?'

Kelby looked innocent. 'She *is* our photographer. I don't know why you're looking so surprised about this. I've been mailing you about it all week!'

'I saw the subject heading and thought you were joking.'

'And Lu didn't mention it to you?'

Will frowned. 'I think she did. I said something about it being a stupid-ass idea and that anyone associated with it was stupid...she hasn't mentioned it again.'

'I can't imagine why,' Kelby said dryly.

Will's mouth flattened. 'I'm really not happy about this.'

'Lucky for you that I don't give a toss whether you're happy about it or not. It's her job.'

Right.

'Where are they doing the shoot?' Will demanded.

'In the gym.' Kelby stood up as Will whipped around and headed for the door. 'Will, don't you dare go down there! Don't make things difficult...'

Kelby sank back into his chair as Will ignored his order. *Friends? Yeah, right!* He hoped that Will didn't make the shoot difficult for Lu, but he wouldn't bet money on it. Kelby lumbered to his feet. Maybe he'd wander down to the gym for a little bit of light entertainment...

She needed a fan. She needed a walk-in fridge. She needed to stop blushing, Lu thought as fifteen briefs-clad, buff, super-sexy rugby players streamed into the Rays' gym, their second home. Will was standing off to one side, fully clothed in jeans and a T-shirt, and the scowl on his face was as black as a summer thundercloud.

He'd yet to say a word to her.

Boxers, briefs, even a set of Y-fronts... *Good grief, Lu, you can't look there!* Was the air-con working down here? The team members weren't fazed about lounging around in their underwear. They chatted and joked and insulted each other about the size of their tackle and the state of their underpants.

'We'll let Lu decide,' Matt hooted.

Lu lifted her eyebrows. 'Decide on what?'

'Boxers, briefs or thongs,' Matt explained. 'What do women prefer?'

Lu kept her face blank, knowing that they were trying to get a reaction. She knew boys—they'd push her until they got one. She hadn't raised twin boys and had all their friends using her house as a second home for nothing. But she couldn't look at Will, because then he'd know that she preferred commando.

Actually, just him buck naked would do the trick.

Matt snapped his fingers under her nose. 'Lu! Concentrate, here—this is important research!'

Lu reached up and patted his cheek. 'Sweetie...trust

me. If I liked you enough to get to the point of wanting to rip your underwear off I wouldn't really care what you were wearing. Though I'd have second thoughts if you were wearing a red thong with black lace...that's just tacky.'

Matt placed his hand on her cheek and his eyes twinkled with fun. 'But you'd like a leopard print thong, right?'

Lu laughed and played along. 'Absolutely! Who can resist a man in a leopard print thong?'

Matt put his thumbs into his black boxers and shimmied them down his hips. Lu slapped her hands over her face and peeked out through her fingers as Matt did a slow turn, wearing nothing more than the briefest, tackiest, fakest leopard print thong.

Lu dropped her hand and bellowed with laughter as Matt posed in front of her, his hip thrust out in a typical model pose. She clapped before placing the back of one hand on her forehead and pretending to swoon.

The room roared. Matt high-fived her and Lu was still laughing when Will stepped away from the wall and cleared his throat. Cold eyes drilled through her and her laughter died in her throat as the room fell into an uncomfortable silence.

He jerked his head at the gym door. 'Outside.'

Lu frowned. 'Sorry?'

'I want to talk to you...outside,' Will stated, in a biting voice vibrating with anger.

'Lu's in trub-bel,' Matt sang, and then winced when Will walked up to him and slammed his hand against Matt's chest. Matt took two steps backwards.

'If you know what's good for you, you'll shut up,' Will stated calmly, his eyes spitting.

Matt held his hands up. 'Yes, boss.'

'You—outside.'

Will looked at Lu and his furious expression had Lu climbing down from the table and walking towards the door. She heard the door slam behind her and looked up at Will, who was obviously thundercloud angry. What was his problem?

'Stop flirting with Matt,' Will stated through clenched teeth.

Wha-at?

'Jeez, Will, he was just trying to make the situation less awkward,' Lu replied, confused. He couldn't be taking their banter seriously, could he? 'What *is* your problem?'

Will stepped in front of her and pushed her back against the wall. He placed a palm on the wall next to her head and loomed over her. 'My problem? You're about to get fifteen guys naked and the only one I want you to see naked is me. *That's* my problem. I'm frustrated and as horny as hell. That's another problem. I don't care if this is your job. I. Don't. Like. It.'

It was the first time she'd seen Will totally stripped of the cloak of control he constantly wore. His eyes were full of misery and frustration. His body was clenched with tension. He looked almost unhinged.

Over *her* being surrounded by hot, buff men... Well, shoot!

As much as she wanted to smash her mouth against his and be kissed by this out-of-control Will, she had a job to do—a job that was important to her. The other rugby franchises, as Kelby had told her, were hiring big-name photographers to capture their images for the calendar, but he had faith in her that she wouldn't let their side down.

She had no intention of doing that, but she couldn't do it with Will hovering like an angry tornado; he'd make the players tense, they wouldn't relax while he was watching over them, and she wouldn't be able to function. She had to get rid of him. Yet she knew that nothing shy of a dynamite stick would get him to leave.

So Lu stood on her tiptoes, slammed her mouth against his and slid her tongue into his mouth. Her kiss was open-mouthed and hot enough to drain all the blood from his brain...just what she needed. It took all her will-power to step away before Will caught her in his grip and wouldn't let her go.

Stepping back quickly, she gave him a quick salute, slipped through the door to the gym, slammed it closed and turned the lock. Ignoring his furious fist pounding against the door, she walked back inside and went to the box she'd carried in earlier and yanked out an i-Pod and external speakers.

'Who wants music?' she asked loudly.

'Yes! But a drink would be better!' Matt responded above a chorus of approval and whistles.

Lu grinned as she pulled two bottles of tequila from the box and waved them in the air. 'I also think this would be a lot easier with a couple of shots. There are quite a few bottles, so don't be shy. But we'd better get slammed *before* Mr Grumpy breaks down the door!'

* * *

Lu, dressed in a brief pair of cycling shorts, a crop top and trainers, stood in front of the punching bag in the empty Rays gym and looked down at the small pair of boxing gloves that Will had just tied onto her hands.

'I tried to book a private lesson for you at a Thai kickboxing school with one of Kelby's mates who is an instructor, but they have a couple of cage fights coming up so he's swamped,' Will told her, dropping her hands. He stepped away from her to get some distance. She was wearing little more than underwear, and his boys weren't making the distinction between gym clothes and lingerie.

It had been a week since he'd held her in his arms, and he'd never be able to look at the sea again without remembering how responsive she'd been to his touch. He'd had a lot of sex over the years, but even the thought of Lu far exceeded the hottest, craziest sex he'd had before.

It was shocking to realise that he, King of Brief Flings, could think like this. He was a rational adult male. He knew that great sex never lasted for ever. It went from great to good, then to OK, and then it faded to *blah* and then to mechanical.

It would happen even with Lu.

Lu interrupted his thoughts. 'Right—gloves on, punch bag waiting.'

Her small hand ploughed into the bag and it drifted ever so slightly. 'That wasn't so good.' She frowned. 'When you hit it, it swings!'

Will grinned. 'That's because I'm lot stronger than you and also because you punch like a girl.'

'Fist into bag. That was a punch,' Lu protested.

'A *girl* punch. You need to put some body weight behind it,' Will told her. 'Stand with your feet shoulder width apart, bend your knees. OK, good. Make a loose fist with each hand and lift, elbows straight out behind you. That's it. Now, push off with your back foot and rotate your wrist and shoulder as you throw the punch.' Will watched as her fist connected with the bag and rocked. 'Better than before.'

'This is hard,' Lu muttered as she tried again.

'Keep your wrist straight. Push off your back foot.' Girl punching still, Will thought, but, seeing the determined look on her face, he knew that she would get it right if it killed her. Lu, he was coming to realise, had the determination of a dung beetle and the stubbornness of a mule.

'When do I learn to kick?' Lu demanded, huffing.

'When you've learned how to punch,' Will told her. 'Keep your other hand up to guard your face. Don't leave your face vulnerable to attack.'

'Who's going to hit me?' Lu demanded.

'If you are going to learn, then do it properly.'

Lu pulled a tongue at him and rocketed her fist into the bag , making it sway harder than before.

'Better.'

After twenty minutes Lu rested her hands on her thighs and looked up at the bag. 'I could've done with one of these when my folks died.'

It was the first time she'd willingly mentioned their death and Will fought not to react, waiting for her to talk. 'There were days when I was so sad and so angry that I used to punch my bed. This is better.'

Will walked over to the fridge next to the mat, pulled out a bottle of water, cracked the lid and held it to Lu's lips. She drank and sank to the mat, crossing her legs as she sat down.

Will joined her and they sat in silence for a while before he asked another question that he'd been wondering about. 'Who told you? About the accident?'

'Mak. He was our next-door neighbour at the time.'

'How did you cope?' Will asked.

'What do you mean?' Lu asked, giving him a blank look.

'Lu, you were a teenager and suddenly responsible for two kids. How did you deal with your parents' deaths? With having your life splattered against a wall?'

Lu was silent for a long time, her eyes on her shoes. 'Strange...nobody has ever asked me that before.'

'You're kidding?'

She bit her bottom lip. 'Nope. People would ask if I was OK but would barely wait for an answer before demanding to know how the twins were coping, whether they were getting counseling, how sad it was that they were orphaned so young.'

Will's heart cracked at the pain coating her words. 'You were also orphaned.'

'But I wasn't eight and blond and cute,' Lu replied.

'So how did *you* cope?' Will repeated his question.

Lu shrugged. 'I don't know, actually. The first six months were a bit of a blur. We cried a lot. I remember that. I also remember doing a lot of exercise with the boys—playing soccer with them, taking them to the beach, making them as tired as possible so that we could all just sleep without dreaming, trying to avoid the nightmares.'

'The boys had nightmares?'

'Not so much.'

'You?'

'Constantly.'

Will lifted his hand and rubbed his thumb along one prominent cheekbone, then he brushed the violet shadows under her eyes. 'Are the nightmares back, Lu?'

'No.'

'But you're not sleeping?' He could see the start of a lie, an excuse, then saw her pull it back and opt for the truth.

'No, not much.'

Will knew that he wasn't stupid when it came to women; he knew that Lu was thinking. She just wasn't as good at hiding it as he was. He'd noticed the way her eyes lingered on his lips, caught the shudder of attraction when he brushed past her. He suspected that, like him, she lay awake at night remembering the feel of naked skin, the warmth of lips and the heat of hands.

Dangerous thoughts...

Will pulled back and jumped to his feet before reaching down and pulling Lu to her feet. 'Punch that bag for another twenty minutes and I guarantee that you'll sleep well tonight.'

'I don't want to sleep.' The words flew out of her mouth and she didn't know where they'd come from. Maybe it was because she felt so at ease with him, so connected. 'One night. That's it. In the morning we go back to being friends, pretend it didn't happen.'

Will's eyes widened in surprise. He wasn't sure if he was hearing what he thought he was hearing. 'What?'

'You—me—bed. In the morning we go back to normal. What do you think?'

Will's eyes heated. 'I should say no...'

Lu's eyes sparked dangerously. 'I swear, if you say no I will punch you so hard you'll never recover!'

Will threw up his hands. 'Peace! My blood just rushed south. I can't think. Except to say...yes! And thank God.'

'Better,' Lu replied, trying to yank her gloves off with her teeth. 'Get these off me so that I can put my hands on you.'

Will stopped just outside of her reach. 'Do *not* touch me, Lu.'

Lu gaped at him. 'What? Why?'

'You touch me and we won't get outside this room,' Will muttered, then grabbed a glove and started pulling at its strings. 'Seriously, Lu, no touching. Yet.'

Lu flushed. All over.

She waved her hands, agitated. 'Hurry!'

As Will roared up to her gate Lu scrabbled in her bag, looking for the keyring that held the remote control to her electric gate.

'Hurry,' Will whispered, his hand hot and high on her thigh.

'Where *is* the damn thing?' Lu demanded.

'Lu, you're killing me here.' Will grabbed her bag and tipped it upside down so that the contents scattered over her lap. 'You women carry around a lot of junk.'

Lu slapped her hand against her forehead. 'Side

pocket!' Fumbling with the bag, she opened the side pocket, yanked out her keys and pointed the remote in the vague direction of the gate. As soon as there was enough space to manoeuvre his Range Rover through the opening Will floored the accelerator and then screeched to a halt and parked the car in a spare space in the garage. The garage door automatically shut behind them and Will groaned as he turned to her.

'I really don't know if I can walk inside.'

Turning, spilling the contents of her bag onto the floor, she clasped his jaw and nipped his mouth, her tongue making tiny forays into his mouth. 'Would it help if I came over there and climbed all over you?' she murmured against his mouth.

Will groaned. 'Yes. Would it help you?'

'So much.'

Will shoved his seat back as Lu scooted across the console and straddled Will's knees.

'Love the fact this is a big car.'

Will pushed a button and his chair flattened out. 'Me too.'

He captured her roving hands and his expression was serious when he looked up at her. 'Lu...stop. Wait... just for a second.'

Lu's hands stilled and then bunched in frustration. 'What?'

'I want you so much, and if you stop this I swear I'll die, but you've got to know...understand. I'm leaving soon—going back to my life in En Zed. I can't get emotionally involved. Love, commitment...us...is not part of the deal. So this would be...'

'A one-time thing. I know. I said that! Suggested it,'

Lu said, licking the tendon that ran down the side of his neck. 'I get it, Will. One night... In the morning we go back to...before.'

'One night. Do you want to go inside?'

'I can't wait that long,' Lu muttered, and Will nodded his agreement.

His hand slid under the loose shirt she'd pulled over her cropped exercise top and he pulled all the garments up and over her head, tossing them onto the passenger seat. Then his thumbs slid across her nipples and all hell broke loose.

Their lips collided and they fought for domination of the kiss. Will shoved his fingers down the back of her pants and pushed her over him as he dropped his mouth to her bare breast. Lu forgot where she was as she ground herself onto his steel hard erection, desperate to have him inside her, to be around him.

Will lifted his head from her chest and yanked his shirt over his head. With Lu's help, he slid his shorts out from under him. Lu, deciding they were taking too long, balanced on one foot and shucked her shorts and panties. Barely giving Will time to cover himself with a condom, she climbed back on him, took him in hand and guided him into her. Groaning as he stretched and filled her, she tucked her face into his neck and inhaled, desperate to use every sense to experience the essence of loving him.

She could feel the banked tension in his hand as he gripped her thighs, the urgency in his tongue as he looked for and found her mouth. She felt him quiver inside her. Needing him, she bore down and clenched her internal muscles.

She couldn't slow this down...didn't want to...besides they had all night. They could explore each other later...

Will started to buck beneath her and she grabbed his shoulders so as not to topple off. He bit his lip, lifted his hips and launched himself deeper into her. She pushed down, determined to be the one to make him lose control.

Harder, higher, deeper, faster. Their world receded and the only question of importance was who was going to come first. Lu whimpered and Will shouted as their worlds exploded. Neither could tell where one started or the other ended, yet both claimed the victory of making the other lose control first, for giving their one-night lover as much pleasure as they possibly could in a large but still cramped car in a dark garage at the end of a summer's day.

The next morning Lu felt Will leave her bed and opened one eye to watch him walk, beautifully naked, to her *en-suite* bathroom, picking up yesterday's clothes on his way. She glanced at her bedside clock and saw that it was a quarter to five. She knew that Will had a beach run with his squad scheduled for six.

It was morning and her one spectacularly glorious night with Will was over. Lu buried her head in her pillow as she heard the shower being turned on and tried not to imagine his beautiful body slick with soap. She'd had sex before—not a lot—but nothing could have prepared her for a night spent with Will. He'd turned to her time and again and each time he'd taught her something new about her body. She hadn't known that she had a spot on her ankle which, when he nibbled it, shot sparks up her legs. Or that the backs of her knees were ticklish and that she melted when he dug his strong fingers into the muscles of her butt. He'd been a tender but demanding lover, and she knew that when she stood up she'd discover that she had aches in places she hadn't known had muscles.

Her suggestion of one night had just bubbled out of her, Lu thought. Probably because she'd felt so emotionally connected to him. For the first time she hadn't just discussed her parents' death but *her* reaction to that news—how she'd coped, how she'd felt. Not how Nate and Daniel had felt. It had been all about her—Lu. He'd cared, sympathised and empathised. If she could have crawled into him and curled up inside him she wouldn't have felt safer.

And *boom!* She had known that she didn't want to go one more day without knowing what his skin tasted like, how those long muscles felt under her hands and whether making love with him would be as magical as she imagined it to be.

It had been all that. And so much more.

Lu heard the shower switched off and turned her back to the door. She told herself that it was morning, that she couldn't ask him to come back to bed. That wasn't the deal. Lu bit her bottom lip as the bathroom door opened and minutes later she felt his weight on the bed and his hand on her shoulder.

She'd tucked the sheet up around her arms, so she knew she was decent when she rolled over and looked at him, his face serious in the half-light of morning. She could see that he was looking for words, that he—

like her—was fighting temptation. She could see it in the heat of his eyes, in the tension of his jaw.

Lu forced herself to shake her head. 'We can't, Will. This is all we get.'

Will bent down and rested his forehead on her shoulder. Lu got a whiff of soap and toothpaste.

'I—'

Lu permitted herself one brief stroke over his hair before dropping her hand. She forced the words out. 'One night, Will. That was the deal. You're going home in six weeks or so. I'm staying here. We're good friends. Let's not spoil it. Complicate it.'

Will kissed her shoulder before straightening. He cupped her cheek in his hand and shook his head. 'Thank you for the best night of my life. You were magnificent.'

'You weren't so bad yourself,' Lu replied, and then she dropped her eyes and forced herself to be practical. 'There's a spare set of keys with a remote for the gate on the rack of hooks next to the fridge. You can let yourself out and I'll get the keys back from you later...at work.'

Will stood up, put his hands on his hips. His lips twisted. 'Well, that was direct.'

She had to be or she'd cry. Or beg him to stay.

'Before I go...no regrets?'

Lu shook her head. 'None.'

'Are we back to normal?'

'Yes,' Lu replied and watched as he sent her a quick smile before leaving her room. She flopped back onto the pillow and stared at the ceiling.

They were back to normal. Whatever *normal* meant.

NINE

——

Will glanced across his car. Lu was curled up in the over-large passenger seat, her head tucked into the space between the seat and the door. She was fast asleep. He glanced at the red lights of the dashboard clock. It didn't matter that it was eleven on a Sunday morning; he'd learnt that Lu could only keep her eyes open for about thirty minutes in a car before falling asleep.

In only a month, along with learning of her propensity to fall asleep in a car, he'd learnt a lot about her—including the fact that she hated peanut butter, loved any decorating show on TV, and that if she was deeply immersed in a book a nuclear bomb could go off next to her and she wouldn't flinch.

She kept her promises and took the one she'd made to her brothers seriously. She was now—thanks to him—sort of able to surf, and he'd taught her to ride a dirt bike. Of course she'd nearly hit a tree on her first attempt, but she'd tried.

As hard as he'd begged—and he'd begged a lot—

she still refused to skydive, and they'd vowed not to go back to pottery lessons.

He still wanted her more than ever. He wanted her in his bed, in his life, in his head. Possibly in his heart. Oh, he knew that it was impossible, but now and again he put aside his fears and resolutions and thought about how good they would be together, imagined a life with her in it. It was his own fairytale—one he knew would never come true.

He liked her—a lot—but he was not emotionally attached to her. He could still walk away.

Lu yawned and stretched and sent him a sleepy look. 'How long have I been asleep?'

'An hour and fifteen,' Will told her.

Lu sat up straight and looked out of the window. 'Where are we? Jeez, I thought we were going to lunch, not travelling halfway up Africa.'

'What is it with you Durbanites? You think that a five-minute drive is too far and you slept for most of the trip. Besides, you'll thank me,' Will replied, switching lanes so that he could take the exit.

Lu pulled her bag onto her lap and took out a small toiletry purse which she quickly opened. Slicking some nude lipstick onto her fabulous mouth, she smacked her lips and Will groaned. He wished she wouldn't do things like that.

Knowing that he might have little time left with her, he wanted to have as much of her as possible. He should warn Lu that he might be leaving sooner than had been planned, but he was unsure what to say. He was also seriously considering Kelby's offer of another six months and then the head coach position.

That being said, he owed the other teams a face-to-face meeting, to listen to their offers, which meant a trip back home and soon.

And if he stayed in Durban what would he do about Lu? Would he want to continue this knowing that he was falling deeper into...*something*...every week he spent with her?

Maybe it was better to keep quiet about his plans until he knew exactly what he was doing and where he was going.

Lu flicked him a small frown. 'Are you OK?'

'Sure...just horny.'

Will almost laughed at the shocked look on her face, but he felt as if there was a boa constrictor wrapped around his hips. He was so *over* being around her and not being able to touch her.

'Wha...?'

'Just because we don't touch or kiss doesn't mean that I don't want you. And when you push your chest out like you were doing and fiddle with your lips it makes me hot.' Will shrugged and looked at his GPS, grateful to have something else to focus on besides his straining shorts. 'We're turning off onto a dirt road coming up on the right. Keep your eyes open for it.'

'Ah...OK.'

Will smiled to himself. She looked flushed and bothered and not nearly as composed as she had been five minutes ago. *Good*. It was about time that someone else in this car felt hot and flustered and on edge. *Welcome to my world, Mermaid*.

Enjoying himself, Will thought he'd push her buttons a little more.

'Of course whatever you do makes me hot,' he said as he pulled off the secondary road onto the dirt road.

'You still want to sleep with me?' Lu said in a choked voice.

'Sleep? Hell, no, I don't want to *sleep* with you. Kiss you everywhere, touch you everywhere, be inside you... yes.' Will pulled into a makeshift parking lot under some large tropical trees and switched off the engine. He lifted his hand from the gear stick to close Lu's open mouth gently.

'But I thought we weren't...'

'I agreed to one night—not to stop wanting you, Lu. Do you think I heard *one night only* and turned into a eunuch?' Will rolled his eyes. 'Don't look so shocked.'

'I'm not sure what to say,' Lu said as he jumped down to the sandy, grass-splattered ground.

She sat statue-still in the passenger seat as he walked around the car to open her door for her. He'd floored her. He could see that. She hopped down from the high cab with a dazed look on her face, and the devil sitting on his shoulder urged him to give her even more to think about.

There was nothing but dense bush on the passenger side, and the Range Rover's over-large body would screen them from arriving cars or anyone walking back to their car.

Grabbing her hand, he jerked her towards him. She opened her mouth to protest and he swooped inside, his tongue finding hers in a long, slow, wet, sexy slide. He felt her murmur into his mouth, a little feminine sound of approval, and he pressed her back against the car door.

'Do you know how much I want you?'

Will grabbed her hand, opened her fingers and placed her open palm on his erection, sinking back towards her mouth. As her thumb brushed over his tip he slipped his hand down her hip and up and under the short, flouncy, sexy sundress she was wearing. His hand smoothed over her bare butt and traced the line of her thong. He stroked her intimately before pulling back to place his hands under her bottom, lifting her up so that he rubbed her intimately, possessively.

Lu let out a yelp that was part surprise and mostly desire as he thrust against her, only a couple of layers separating him from utter perfection.

'God...' Will muttered against her neck, tasting the dent in her collarbone. 'I could take you right here, right now.'

Lu nipped his lower lip and then licked the bite of pain away. 'And I'd let you.'

Will rested his forehead against hers. 'You're driving me insane, Lu. We're going to have to do something about this, Mermaid, before I explode from sexual frustration. We're adult enough to have this— do this—without getting our fingers burnt.'

In his head, *spontaneous* was currently wiping the floor with *control's* face and Will didn't really care.

'We both know what this is—a short-term, big-fun fling. Let's take the risk!'

'Jeez, Will. What happened to sex and I walk, etcetera, etcetera?'

Will shrugged and looked at her with eyes of liquid gold. 'C'mon, Lu, let's live a little.'

Lu's mermaid eyes widened in shock. *'Now?'*

Will grinned as he let her slide to her feet. 'No, not now. I'd prefer to do it without an audience.'

'*What?*' Lu screeched whipping around in shock to see who was watching them.

Will shouted his laughter and gestured to his left with his thumb. A small troupe of monkeys sat in a grassy clearing, watching them, heads cocked and seemingly fascinated by their antics.

Lu let out an enormous sigh of relief and put her hand on her chest. 'You skunk, Will! I nearly had heart failure!'

Will grinned and leaned his shoulder into the car door as he watched the monkeys scamper back into the bush.

In the ladies' bathroom—in Lu's opinion very conveniently situated at the entrance of whatever this place was—Lu splashed cold water on her face in order to bring down the ferocious colour in her cheeks.

In the mirror above the sink her wide, wild eyes blazed back at her, and she thought that anyone with half a brain would realise that if she didn't get Will into bed again soon she would spontaneously combust.

She'd never, ever experienced such heat and passion before. Every time she and Will touched they went from friends to frenetic in a heartbeat. She wanted him, and he very obviously wanted her, and he was right. They were going to have to do something about it soon.

They were kidding themselves if they thought they could continue this farce about friendship. They'd tried hard, but this compulsion to get naked was too big for both of them. Forget one night—she'd take all the nights she could get, and there weren't that many of them left.

But she had to try and be sensible too—think through how she could be his lover and still wave him goodbye in the not so distant future. He could have her body, do what he wanted with it, but she had to find a way to make sure that when he left her behind he didn't take her heart and soul with him.

Who knew how she was actually going to achieve that? But she'd survived her parents' death, raising her brothers, and she'd damn well do this too. Because— as she was coming to realize—independence wasn't just about a career and learning to live on her own. It was also about making decisions, sticking with them and dealing with the consequences of those choices.

That was independence of thought, a liberation of her spirit, a choice that was all hers. And she was choosing Will, for as long as she could have him.

She didn't know what the cost of this decision would be, but she'd pay the price life demanded and she'd be fine.

Because she was, if nothing else, a survivor.

Lu downed half a glass of icy wine, caught Will's eye and blushed again. She placed the palm of her hand on her forehead and closed her eyes against his wicked, laughing amber eyes. 'You are a bad man, Will Scott.'

Will leaned forward and dropped his voice. 'A *very* bad man.'

Lu blushed again and groaned. 'Will you stop now? Please? I am *so* embarrassed!'

Will just grinned and sipped his beer.

Lu picked up her glass again, took another reviving sip and looked around. She felt beach sand under her sandals, slipped her feet out of them and dug her toes in. There were about ten rickety tables planted in the sandy dune, a rough-looking bar, and a lot of people were either seated at the tables or hanging around the bar. Some were sitting in enormous baskets hanging from a massive wild fig tree, others were seated on beach blankets. Everyone was barefoot, some women wore bikinis, and a lot of the men were shirtless.

'OK, so where are we?'

Will sipped his beer directly from an icy bottle. 'The Beach Shack. Fresh seafood, caught this morning...'

Lu's grin was wide. 'I've always wanted to come here. This is great! It really does look like a shack.'

'But it has the best seafood anywhere, or so I am told,' Will said, leaning so far back in his chair that its front legs lifted off the sand. 'Kelby told me about this place.'

'It reminds me of some of the places my parents used to whip us off to when I was a kid. Sunday lunches were something we always did...fancy hotels, rickety restaurants, diners, dives. We visited them all. My parents always knew where the best food was.' Lu's eyes clouded over and her voice dropped. She was back in that place of tough memories and spiky pain. She shook it off. 'We had our last lunch with them about three weeks before they died. A really expensive lunch. I remember that my mom tried to pay with her credit card and there was a problem. Dad used three cards before the charge went through. That should've been a big clue.'

Will's chair hit the ground. He leaned forward and his eyes were sympathetic when they met hers. 'They were struggling? Financially?'

'Struggling? No. They were to all intents and purposes bankrupt.' Lu drained her glass and tried to change the subject. He didn't need to know this. She shouldn't share it. Sex was one thing, but connecting with him over her very emotional past was just stupid—especially since she was trying to keep her emotional distance. 'The sea is just over this dune, I take it?'

'Down that path.' Will nodded to a thin track that snaked over the dune and reached for her hand. He rubbed his thumb over her wrist. 'Talk to me, Lu.'

'Can we take a walk? Would they keep our table?' Lu asked as she stood up. Will followed her to his feet and nodded. 'I'm sure they will. Let's go.'

Will took her hand in his and led her up and over the dune, not pressuring her to talk—which she appreciated. The sea pounded the beach and washed over their feet. Will just held her hand in his big one.

'After they died I never gave finances another thought,' Lu said eventually, lifting her face up to the hot sun. 'The insurance policies paid out really quickly and there was so much money; the policies were *huge*. The irony is that my parents wouldn't have been able to afford the premiums the next month.'

Lu stopped, bent down to pick up a cowry shell and absently handed it to Will, placing it into the palm of his free hand. She didn't notice when Will slipped it into the pocket of his cargo shorts.

'I hired a financial advisor and he moved the money around—put it into high-interest-bearing funds and accounts. My focus was on the boys, so I was so grateful for his help. Still am.'

'How did you find out that they were broke?' Will asked.

'About six months after they died I finally had enough distance, enough strength, to clean out their closets, the study, sort through their personal stuff.'

'I keep forgetting that you were still a teenager when you did all this,' Will said, and Lu heard the pain in his voice...for *her*.

'There were boxes of unpaid, unopened bills. Boxes and boxes of papers that they should have paid attention to. I opened them all and I felt...devastated all over again. And so, so guilty.'

Will squeezed her hand and the pain and guilt took a step back. 'Why guilty, Lu?'

'Because my parents died in order for us to live this very comfortable life.' Lu stared down at her bare feet. 'If they'd lived our lives would've been very different. No fancy schools or university for the boys. Now there's enough money for them to start a business or buy a house later on.'

'Did they leave the money to your brothers?'

'No. It was equally divided.'

'Then why do you talk as if this is the twins' inheritance and not yours?'

Good question. She *did* do that—think that. 'I don't know. Maybe it's because I was an adult—legally, at least—when they died, and therefore had had the benefit of a life with them. They hadn't.'

'You were also the one who put your entire life on hold to look after them. You are as entitled to your share of the money as they are.'

'They lost their parents, Will,' she objected.

'Sweetheart, so did you.' Will placed his hands on her shoulders and squeezed. 'They only had to deal with their grief. You had to deal with a lot more.'

'My parents must have been so incredibly scared—desperate about what they were going to do. How they were going to look after the boys. Where they were going to live. And even more scary the loss of their image and lifestyle and friends.' Lu dug her toes into the wet sand and blinked furiously. 'Accommodation, food, car, petrol…all my big expenses are paid for by the trust, but I feel like I can't use any of the money on me, on things I'd like.'

'Why not?'

Lu linked her hands behind her head and looked at Will with huge, haunted eyes.

Will touched her cheek with the tips of his fingers. 'Lu, you can't punish yourself for something they did or didn't do. They made the decision not to look after their finances, not you,' Will insisted. 'As for using the money—let's look at the situation another way, Lu. If just one of your parents had died the other would've have had to hire an *au pair* to help with the twins. Am I right?'

'Yes.'

'And that *au pair* would've been paid?'

'Yes.'

'It's a basic analogy, and nowhere near what you did for the boys, but my point is still the same. Use the money, Lu. No guilt attached.' Will slung an arm around her shoulders and hauled her to his side. He dropped a kiss on her temple. 'If you used your share of the money now, would it change the fact that they were broke?'

'No.'

'Would it bring them back?'

'No.' Lu put her hand around Will's broad back and held on tight.

Will looked down at her and touched her chin with the tips of his fingers. 'Then use the money, sweetheart.' He pulled off his cap and placed it over Lu's head. 'I think it's time we got that gorgeous face of yours out of the sun. I can see the freckles forming as we speak.'

Lu yelped, slapped a hand over her nose.

Will laughed. 'I'm joking, Mermaid. When is it going to sink into your head that I *like* your freckles?'

Will shut and locked the front door behind him, and Lu dropped her bag onto the floor in the hall and kicked off her sandals. Their lunch at The Beach Shack had rolled on into the afternoon and early evening. Like a lot of the other patrons they'd gone back to the beach and watched the sun set over the Indian Ocean, and it had been fully dark when they'd finally made the long trip home.

She'd fallen asleep in the car on the way back. Again.

Lu walked into the kitchen, opened the fridge door

and pulled out two bottles of water. She tossed one to Will, who caught it with one hand. He cracked the lid and watched her with hooded eyes as he downed half the contents in one long swallow. The entire day had been one long foreplay session, starting with that sexy interplay against the car door. While he had been careful to keep his hands off her all day—most of the patrons at the restaurant had known exactly who he was, and a couple of mobile cameras had been used—she'd seen the heat in his gaze and his whispered words had had her blood bubbling.

'I love the veins on the inside of your wrist. Can you feel my lips on them?'

'I'm imagining you in my bed, all long legs and a sexy smile.'

Lu ran the icy bottle down her neck and watched Will's eyes flare.

A muscle jumped in his jaw as he replaced the cap on the water bottle. 'Hot, Lu?'

'It's summer in Durban,' Lu replied, and couldn't believe her voice could sound so raspy, so sexy. Emboldened, she rolled the bottle against her chest, let it drift across her nipples.

'If you're that hot, then I have an idea.'

Will grabbed her hand, yanked her towards the veranda doors and quickly unlocked them. Pulling her into the still hot night, he led her down the veranda steps to the dark pool. He lifted his hands and held her slim neck.

'Making out with you in the pool has been a big fantasy of mine.'

'Making out? Is that all we're going to do?' Lu asked as he used his thumbs on her jaw to tip her head up.

'I hope not,' Will groaned, just before his mouth fell onto hers.

Lu had expected hot and crazy, but she got slow and sexy—a deliberate, tantalising exploration of every inch of her mouth: a lick here, a nip there. His hands drifted down to her back, deftly unzipping the small zip that held her sundress together. The dress fell in a frothy pile at her feet and she stood in her strapless bra and tiny thong in the moonlight, her body his for the taking.

His big hands smoothed a path down her spine, over her bare buttocks, over the tops of her thighs. They traced her ribcage and slid from her shoulders to her fingers, leaving her nerve-endings quivering.

'So beautiful,' Will muttered.

Right now, she actually believed him. Lu pushed her hands up and under his T-shirt, urging him to take it off. Will lifted his hand, grabbed the back of the shirt behind his neck and yanked it off in that very masculine way of his. Lu groaned as she felt those long muscles vibrating with tension under her hands. Why had she waited so long to touch him again, to taste his skin, to experience the utter wonder of Will?

Lu gasped as his fingers unsnapped the buttons of his shorts and he pushed them and his boxers down his hips. He stood in front of her, bare-ass naked. In the low light spilling from the house he looked like every woman's fantasy. Strong and tall and proud, broad shoulders, rippled stomach, lean hips, and she couldn't ignore his obvious and very large erection.

It was just for her, and she couldn't wait to play with him.

'That's a very naughty smile, Lu,' Will said softly, his hands going to her hips.

'I was having a very naughty thought, Will,' Lu responded.

'I like naughty thoughts.' Will put his finger on her skin and pulled at the fabric between her breasts. 'As much as I like this, I'd prefer it off.'

Lu spun around and offered him her back. 'Feel free.'

Will unhooked her bra, dropped it to the ground and placed his mouth at the top of her spine as his hands cupped both her breasts. His thumbs rubbed her nipples, pulling them up into hard pebbles as his erection nestled into her butt.

'Walk,' he whispered in her ear. 'Into the pool. I have a fantasy to make true.'

Lu settled down into the corner of her couch to watch the Saturday night movie, a bowl of popcorn in her lap, Dore tucked in behind her knees. This was the first night she'd spent alone for more than a week and the house felt empty without Will.

She'd loved every second of having him around.

Every. Second.

He sang in the shower—mushy Nineties songs, off-key and totally out of tune. It made every day an adventure in 'Guess the Tune'. He'd watched her make red velvet cupcakes and eaten three while she'd waited for them to cool, swiping pieces of cake through the cream cheese icing instead of waiting for her to ice them. They'd gone to the photography exhibition and he had staunchly but erroneously insisted that her work was better.

She'd rewarded him handsomely for that.

And they'd had sex. Lots and lots of lovely, lovely sex.

And because she loved being with him she'd deliberately encouraged him to accept Mak's invitation to a soccer match at the stadium in the city.

She frequently reminded herself that he was just someone she was having fun with—someone who would be leaving soon. A man who'd arrived in her life at a time when she needed a friend—someone to make her laugh, to help her play.

And because it was becoming harder and harder to remember that he was leaving she'd thought a night apart wasn't a bad thing. It would help her to gain some much needed distance, perspective, being a reminder that this insane happiness wasn't permanent.

It was make-believe, pretend...a little romantic escape from real life. If she started to think it was anything else she was setting herself up for a fall.

Ooh, movie starting, Lu thought. Hot hero...not nearly as sexy as Will...but then again who was?

Her mobile rang and she scowled down at it when she saw an unfamiliar number on the screen. She just wanted some time out.

'Hello?'

'Hold for a call please,' a crisp voice instructed her, and she frowned.

'Lu? God, Lu...'

Nate's voice broke and Lu shot up, dislodging the cat as her heart belted up into her throat.

'Nate! What's wrong?' she demanded, her voice croaky with fear.

'We went to a music festival and as we were leaving Daniel and I and a couple of other guys got ambushed. There were about eight guys and they roughed us up. Stole our phones...wallets.'

'Are you hurt? How's Daniel?'

'I'm phoning from the hospital...they admitted him. He got kicked in the head and he won't wake up—'

Nate's voice broke again and she heard the tears in his stutter.

'They say he should. Maybe in a day or so. But, Lu, can you come?'

Lu felt the scream forming in her throat, swallowed it down and looked for the rigid calm that she knew he needed to hear from her. 'Of course. I'll catch the first plane I can. Where are you? Where is *he*?'

'Constantia General. Casualty. I don't have any money...a friend of mine is bringing me a phone, so I'll text you the number when I get it.'

'OK. Keep in touch,' Lu stated, idly noticing that her knee was bouncing and that her hand was shaking. 'And Nate...?'

'Yeah?'

'He will be fine. I promise.'

'Just come, Lu. I'm scared.'

'I know, Nate.' She was terrified beyond belief too, but she had to be strong. For him and for Daniel. 'Hang tough.'

Lu disconnected and stared down at her mobile.

Instinctively she dialled Will's number and wrapped her arm around her middle as she waited for him to answer.

'If this is a booty call, I'm your man...' Will answered on a laugh.

Lu closed her eyes as an involuntary sob escaped.

'Lu...honey? What's wrong? Are you ok?'

'No...' Lu answered, and as if from miles away heard the breath he sucked in. 'I'm fine. Daniel my brother isn't. I need a lift to the airport. I have to get to Cape Town as soon as possible. Can you take me to the airport? I'm shaking too much to drive and I need to try to get a flight...and information from the hospital about his condition...'

'I'm on my way. Leaving now. Hold on, baby. I'm coming.'

Lu rested her mobile against her forehead as tears rolled down her face. She'd known that he'd drop everything, that he'd come running. Just this one time she didn't have to be alone.

TEN

On the late-afternoon flight back
from Cape Town a week later, Lu rested her head
against the window and stared at the clouds below.
She was barely aware of the minor turbulence. Her
thoughts were too full of this past week and the knowl-
edge that she was finally going home...to Will.

He'd been amazing, she remembered. Calm, cool,
so very in control. He'd thrown some clothes into an
overnight bag for her, because she hadn't thought to
pack anything, buckled her into her seat and, while he
raced down the highway, held her hand as she'd called
the airport to book a seat on the midnight flight to
Cape Town. When she'd finally got through to the doc-
tor who had been treating Daniel she'd been shaking
so much that she'd hardly been able to talk, so he'd
taken the phone and got all the relevant information.
Daniel had had minor bleeding under his skull. They
were keeping him sedated to give the swelling time to
subside, he'd told her. He'd taken her credit card and
swiped the automated ticket machine for her, holding

onto her ticket and her until it had been time for her flight to be called.

When it had, he'd calmly boarded the plane with her—she hadn't realised that he'd purchased a ticket for himself as well—and he'd held her through the two-hour flight. She couldn't remember how they'd got to the hospital, just that Will had been there, solid and steadfast at the end of her hand. He'd bought her coffee, hired a car and taken a battered and dinged Nate back to his digs so that he could shower and rest. While Daniel lay statue-still, Will had held her while she wept.

He'd brought Nate back to the hospital and at around midday the next day, when Daniel had started showing signs of improving, Will had kissed her forehead and told her that he'd see her back at home.

She'd stayed in Cape Town for the week and she'd missed him. Ferociously. He'd called often, and while she'd been speaking to him her world had made sense. Her stomach had stopped churning, her breath had evened out and she'd relaxed. For those five, ten, fifteen minutes she'd felt settled, calm, relaxed.

Lu banged her head against the back of her headrest and mentally slapped herself.

She'd tried so hard to keep her emotional distance but she was falling for him. Even worse, was coming to rely on him. She wanted to have the right to call him, wanted to feel that he was the man she could lean on, rely on, love. And how stupid was that? She wanted him for everything: for companionship, friendship, sex, support...and worst of all for love.

When had this happened? *How* had it happened?

She'd been so aware, so on guard, so determined not to allow herself to feel more.

She was *such* a moron.

'*Love, commitment, wasn't part of the deal.*'

Lu heard Will's voice in her head and closed her eyes. *Stupid, stupid girl.*

Anyway, she couldn't afford to rely on him—on anybody—for emotional support because when she did she fell apart.

If she hadn't had Will in her life she would have managed to keep calm, would have called on all that strength she'd learnt in coping with her parents' death, and just put one foot in front of the other and got the job done. But because Will *was* around, so strong and capable, she'd collapsed and allowed him to take over.

What if—God forbid—this happened again when Will was halfway across the world? How would she cope? She wouldn't have a strong shoulder to lean on. Mak was her friend, but he had his own crosses to bear. No, she couldn't allow herself to become weak, to rely on anyone else. To rely on Will.

She had to pull back. She had to put some distance between them. She had to be tough, be a survivor...

After all, she did it so well.

Will's shin slammed into the bag, followed by a fast fist, and he bounced away from the punch bag. Since he'd returned from his very brief visit to Cape Town he'd spent a ridiculous amount of time in this corner, muttering to himself.

He hated, *loathed*, the idea of Lu being on her own in Cape Town, even though Daniel was well on the road to recovery. He'd had to have surgery to pin a broken wrist later in the week and Will had wanted to be with Lu, even though it was just minor surgery. She worried, and he worried about her while she was worrying about them.

Was she eating? Sleeping? Had he done enough for her? Should he have stayed longer? Called more often? Offered to take a couple of days off work to be with her?

Will stepped away from the bag and put his fists on his thighs. He missed her, and speaking on the phone just didn't cut it. He missed her morning smile, waking up in the middle of the night to find her snuggled into his back, her arm around his waist. Damn it, he even missed her house—missed being in it with Lu. He could relax there, could kick back and just think. He could sit on the veranda and watch the ocean, work at her dining table or in her very messy study, lie on her leather couch and watch the sports channels.

Lu gave him space to move, to think, to *be*. Space to be alone but not to be lonely... She didn't prod or pry or make demands for him to give her anything more than what he was currently giving her.

It was fabulous. It was soul-deep petrifying. The fire still raged.

Will knocked his fist against the bag. Was he allowing himself to be seduced by the fairytale? This wasn't like him—wasn't the person who kept an iron grip on his control, his emotions—and he barely recognised himself.

She turned him upside down and inside out with her ability to decimate his control in and out of the bedroom. When he was making love to her he was outside himself, his mind switched off and his body taking over, taking control. With any other woman he would have sprinted away weeks ago, and although he'd thought about it he still hadn't managed to do it. He had decisions to make—career decisions about other franchises who wanted to work with him—and he wished he could talk to Lu about it. But he couldn't, because talking just strengthened the bond between them. He should be trying to break those bonds, not make them stronger. He had to dig deep and end this. The longer he delayed, the more difficult it would be.

He was leaving Durban—leaving her. That was non-negotiable. The fire was at full strength now and he knew that some time in the not too distant future it would start to burn out.

It would end. Soon. Something would happen to douse the flames or he'd leave. And the sooner he got used to that idea, the better.

The next morning Will placed a cup of coffee on the bedside table next to Lu and sighed when she refused to meet his eyes. For most of the previous evening he'd tried to engage her in conversation, but that had been like pulling walrus teeth and he was thoroughly sick of it. For the first time ever they hadn't made love, and Lu had lain in his arms stiff and unresponsive.

'What's going on, Lu?'

Lu didn't meet his eyes. 'Nothing.'

'Bull! You're terse, quiet and irritable.'

'Sorry. I've got a lot on my mind. In case you hadn't noticed, it's been a tough week.'

Ooh, sarcasm. Just what he needed.

'Want to talk about it?' Will asked, knowing what her answer would be. But despite the massive lectures he kept giving himself about stepping back he needed to know what she was thinking, where she was at.

He wanted to stop caring about her—he did. He just hadn't the faintest idea how to do it!

'No, I don't want to talk.'

'Has there been more news from Daniel?' Another question. He was obviously a glutton for punishment.

'No, he's fine. Well, still headachy, but OK.' Lu sat up in bed, picked up her coffee cup and sipped.

'Well, if you're not going to talk to me I might as well just go.'

'I'm just dealing with some stuff, Will.'

'If you're going to deal with it in moody silence I'm not going to watch,' Will snapped.

Something flashed in Lu's eyes that he couldn't identify. Fear? Relief?

'If you don't want to be here, Will, nobody is holding a gun to your head.'

'OK, *that* was bitchy, ' Will shot back. 'Stop shutting me out, Lu.'

'Oh, what? Like you do to me? All the time?'

'What does *that* mean?' he demanded.

Lu climbed out of bed and angled her chin. 'You seem to want to climb inside my head but you won't let me into yours!'

'What do you want to know?' Will asked.

Lu shoved her hands into her hair. 'You *know* what I want to know! I want to know what happened with your marriage. Why you are so anti-relationships! Are you still in love with her?' Lu asked.

'Jo? Hell no!' Will swore under his breath. 'You want to know? Fine—I'll tell you.' He sat down on the edge of the windowsill. 'It was anything but a fairytale. We got married when we were both twenty-two, and during the two years we were hitched I think we just entertained each other.' He raked a hand through his hair. 'We also played hard—far too hard. We had too much money and we thought we were very special. We married in a flurry of sex-fuelled adrenalin and over time the chemistry fizzled. I think if we'd spent more time together it would've fizzled a lot quicker.'

Now came the hard part.

'There were many reasons why it was on a downward slide, but I gave it the killing blow.' *Just spit it out.* 'She caught me cheating. It wasn't the first or the only time I did it, but it was the first time she caught me at it.'

Lu's expression remained neutral but he knew she was good at not reacting. Her eyes gave her away. Was that disappointment he saw? Yep, there it was. Just what he'd expected.

'OK. Carry on.'

'You want more? We allowed, even encouraged each other to walk on the wild side, but that was her line: infidelity. I crossed it. All the time. Probably hoping that she'd catch me at it. She eventually did.'

'Why didn't you just leave her?'

'Because I *liked* being able to say that I was married to one of the world's sexiest women. I was that shallow—that superficial,' Will retorted. 'I wasn't a nice guy, Lu. I'm still not.'

Lu didn't disagree with him and he felt disappointed. Then he got annoyed at himself for feeling disappointed.

'OK, I understand that you had a bad marriage, but why have you avoided relationships?' she asked.

Were they *really* going to discuss this now? Lu had her stubborn face on. Yep, they were. 'Jo was wild and exciting and the sex was crazy. Sex—attraction—fuels love, and when it burns out you are left with a pile of ashes.'

'I disagree with you. I think love fuels sex.'

'Yeah, that's what the fairytales want us to believe. It doesn't work like that. Not for me, anyway. I don't want to be trapped when attraction dies off—having to stay in a relationship because I'm obligated to. I don't trust the spark to last, Lu.'

'That's such a lousy excuse for not being brave enough to take a chance,' Lu stated.

'And you? Are *you* so brave?' Will shot back, needing to launch some arrows of his own. 'Isn't this ice princess act a way to distance yourself from me?'

He knew that he'd hit the target when temper shot into her eyes. 'No, it's you crowding me! Hovering! Will, I've been alone for a long time, and sometimes I'm not sure what to do with you! I just want some time on my own...some time to think!'

'You've had a whole week away from me to think!' He gripped the bridge of his nose and tried to find some control. 'I just wanted to help, Lu.'

He didn't know that those last few words would put a match to the powder keg of her temper.

'I don't *need* your help!' Lu cried. 'I didn't need it when I buried my parents, or when I lay in this bed, with two little boys sobbing their hearts out, one on either side of me. I didn't need it when they had measles, or when Nate got his heart broken. Where were you when I had to turn down every career opportunity I ever received because I had supper to put on the table? I don't *need* your help. I don't need *anyone!*'

Whoa! Will stepped back as her words whipped his soul. 'So why did you call me last week? Why didn't you just cope, Lu?'

'Because I was weak! You're leaving and I can't—*won't*—rely on you or anybody else!' Lu turned away to stare out of the window.

Will slapped his coffee cup onto the bedside table and glared at her stiff back. In his mind a video of a helicopter dumping a scoop of water on a bushfire played. Yet the fire still raged.

'Well, you can have as much time to yourself as you need.'

He was leaving soon anyway. What did he care?

Too much, he thought as he headed down the stairs to her front door. He stopped, leaned his forehead on the wood and told himself to walk through the door.

He cared. *Damn.*

The idea of leading the Rays onto the field was, in theory, a great idea for little Deon, but now that he could hear the forty thousand plus crowd roaring and see the craziness of the tunnel, with officials, medics and members of the press rushing in and out, he was thoroughly overwhelmed.

There was no chance that he'd run out onto the field by himself, Lu realised after trying to talk to him again.

He buried his head in Mak's stomach and refused to let his dad go. Kelby, standing to her left with a representative of the Rays' biggest corporate sponsor, sent her an enquiring look and she drew her hand across her throat.

Mak bent down to speak to Deon again. 'Bud, listen—the Rays are coming up from the dressing room. Look—there's Jabu.'

Deon shook his head and placed his hands over his face. Lu glanced at her watch and winced. In five minutes the opposition would storm onto the field, Deon or not. Both she and Mak knew that he wanted to do it, but he was swamped with fear.

Poor kid. Lu placed her hand on Mak's shoulder and as she did so felt the brief touch of a masculine hand on her back.

'Problem?' Will asked.

Lu looked around and couldn't help the flutter of her heart, the catch in her throat. She hadn't spoken to him since he'd left her house, and avoiding him had been easy this week as he had taken the squad for a team-building session up-country.

She'd felt lost and miserable all week.

Could she have been more horrible, mean, spiteful? She'd asked Will for help and he hadn't asked any questions. He'd jumped into the situation—spent his Saturday night travelling across the country so that she didn't have to be alone—and she'd repaid him by lashing out at him because she was scared of becoming reliant on him.

That was her problem, not his. He'd been honest with her. He hadn't offered anything more than friendship and by helping her, supporting her, he'd given exactly that. She'd repaid that generosity by goading him into telling her about his past, by verbally punching him when he'd offered help.

If the twins had acted like that she would have had more than a couple of words with them.

She had to apologise, and she had to apologise in a way that he'd know meant something. Sometimes words were too easy, but she had to try.

'Will, I—'

Will looked at her and she sighed at his poker face.

'What's the problem?' he asked, nodding at Deon.

'Stage fright,' Lu whispered over Deon's head.

'He can't do this, Will.' Mak looked at Will with agonised eyes.

'Sure he can; he can do anything he wants to do,' Will replied.

The match director lifted his finger to indicate that Deon should get into position and Lu noticed that both teams were lined up behind them in the tunnel—thirty big, burly, determined men.

Will dropped to his haunches and pulled Deon away from Mak, lifted up his face to make eye contact. 'Pretty scary, huh?'

Deon nodded furiously.

'Would you do it if someone went with you?' Will asked gently.

Deon nodded. 'Jabu.'

'Jabu can't do it, sport. He's got to lead the Rays on. That's an important captain's job.' Will smiled reassuringly. 'What about me? I've led a couple of teams onto the field and I kind of know what to do.'

Deon gave him an assessing stare and Lu had to bite her lip to keep from smiling. The kid was actually taking his time to decide whether Will was worthy of the honour. It seemed like an eternity before Deon nodded his head, stepped away from Mak and Lu and slid his small hand into Will's enormous one.

'Can you do this?' Lu hissed her question at him. 'Shouldn't you be somewhere?'

He should be on his way to the coach's box, from where he'd issue instructions to his people on the ground.

Will shrugged as he stood up. 'It's his dream. I can take five minutes to make it come true.'

Lu's eyes softened and she briefly touched his other hand with hers. 'You're a good man, Will Scott.'

Will sent her a small smile, tugged Deon into position, and the next moment they were walking onto the field. Lu's heart tumbled as her huge, sexy lover slowed his long stride so that Deon, holding the game ball, could keep up with him. When the crowd noticed who was on the field they let out a roar of approval and the sound ricocheted around the stadium.

'And it seems like Will Scott is accompanying Deon Sibaya onto the field today.' The commentator's voice skimmed over the crowd noise. 'Deon is the Rays' biggest and most special fan. He's a student at St Clare's in their special needs programme. And, ladies and gentlemen, following them onto the field, please welcome, from Melbourne, the defending champions!'

Oh, good grief. She was inches away from toppling off the I-love-you cliff, from throwing her heart at his feet. He was smart and strong. How could she *not* fall in love with him? He was an exceptional leader, great with kids. A wonderful inspiration to young men who, through him, could realise that life could be turned around, respect could be re-earned.

He was funny and flawed, hot but tender.

And she thought she might be in love with him. It didn't matter that he was leaving shortly, that he might not want to hear the words, she owed it to herself to tell him, to let him know. She also, at the very least, owed him an apology for acting like a brat.

It would mean opening herself up, laying her heart on the line, being vulnerable—but she had to do it. He might not want her love, might not do anything with it, but she didn't want to live with the regret of not telling him how she felt—how special this time had been with him, what an impact he'd had on her life.

Will and Deon had reached a quarter way across the field and Will kept a hand on Deon's shoulder as the opposition milled a few metres from them, bouncing on their toes, some doing hamstring stretches. Deon's eyes were as wide as flying saucers, Lu thought. Leaving Mak, who'd dropped his sunglasses onto his face to hide his tears, she moved to the side of the field and took her camera off her shoulder to shoot the Rays players as they hurtled past her.

'And, ladies and gentlemen, your team—the Stingrays!'

Lu held her finger on the button and hoped that she'd got some decent shots as the team stormed past her. Immediately she swung her camera around to the field, where Jabu ran directly up to Deon and Will and put out his fist for Deon to bump.

Will slapped Jabu on the shoulder and Lu swallowed.

She captured the image and kept shooting as Jabu repeated the gesture with his coach and Will and Deon turned to walk back towards her. When Deon spotted her on the sidelines he broke into a bumbling run, and she dropped her camera to catch him as he jumped into her arms.

'Did'ja see me, Lu? Did'ja?' he demanded.

'You are *such* a superstar,' she told him, and held out her hand as Will walked past her. He captured her fingers in his and squeezed. Lu, oblivious to the massive crowd, the important match that was about to start and the various photographers and officials milling about, looked up at him with star-shiny eyes. 'As for you, Will Scott...'

Will's slow, sexy smile dimpled his cheek. 'As for me what, Mermaid?'

'*You* are simply magnificent,' Lu said simply.

Will stepped closer and, ignoring the bouncing Deon at their feet, caught her chin in his hand and tipped her face up. 'Funny, I was thinking the same thing about you.'

Will brushed his lips across hers in a kiss that was brief but still sent tingles down to her toes. 'Good luck,' she murmured against his mouth.

Will tapped her nose. 'Thanks. Good job, kid.' He ran a hand over Deon's hair. 'I've got a corporate function tonight, but I'll call you later, OK?'

'I'll be waiting.'

ELEVEN

He didn't call. Not that night. And on Sunday morning Lu looked at the Sacher torte she'd made the previous night and decided to deliver it in person. She needed to talk to Will, and the longer she delayed this conversation the easier it was to talk herself out of it.

I'm sorry I was so bitchy. I think that I might be in love with you. I thought that you might like to know.

Lu practised the simple words until she had them word-perfect but she suspected that they would fly away, never to be recaptured, when she actually had to say them to Will, face to face.

Shortly after nine Lu banged on the door to his apartment again and wished he'd hurry and open up. The triple-layer, meticulously crafted Sacher torte she'd made him was rather heavy. Lu knocked again and gnawed the inside of her lip. Maybe he'd changed his mind and was hiding behind the door, hoping she'd go away.

After waiting another couple of minutes with no response, she turned away and walked back to the lift.

Damn, she thought, blinking back tears. She'd thought they'd turned a corner yesterday at the match. She'd seen something in his face that had given her hope.

The doors to the lift were sliding open when he finally yanked open his door. 'Where the hell are you going with that cake?' he demanded.

Lu turned around slowly and sucked in her breath at Will, who was leaning against the frame of the door, a towel around those lean hips. She licked her lips as she walked back towards him. 'I'm holding the cake hostage. Where the cake goes, I go.'

'You drive a hard bargain.' Will stood back and jerked his head for her to come inside. He slammed the door closed behind her. 'Give me a minute to get dressed and I'll make some coffee to go with that cake.'

'I'll make the coffee,' Lu said as she walked into the galley kitchen and deposited the cake on the counter.

Flicking on the kettle, she looked at the empty boxes of Chinese takeaway on the counter. Behind the dustbin was an empty pizza box.

When Will returned to the kitchen, dressed in old jeans and a rugby jersey, she flicked the takeaway boxes with her finger. 'Don't you ever cook for yourself?'

'Nope,' Will replied as he joined her in the small space of the kitchen.

She could smell the soap he'd just used in the shower and peppermint toothpaste. Lu nodded to the stack of papers she'd placed on the narrow counter. 'I brought the papers.'

'Thanks. Sorry I didn't call. The function finished late and I was knackered.'

'No problem.'

She was here, with him, finally. There definitely was a God, Will thought, amazed at how happy he was to see her. They needed to talk today. He needed to tell her of the decisions he had to make, get her input, see what she thought. Lu was an integral part of his life now. He didn't know where they were going, but he owed it to her to talk it through.

He'd have to say things he didn't know how to say— try to explain feelings that he wasn't sure he'd identified yet—find a path he couldn't see yet. Frankly, he'd rather drip hot wax in his eye, but he needed to talk to her.

Because he was so tempted to delay the conversation by taking her to bed, Will stepped backwards. The stack of newspapers fell to the floor and all the sections skidded across the tiles.

Lu looked down at the papers beneath the chair and frowned at the distinctive colours of a Rays shirt on the front page of the society section. 'Ha-ha, some Rays player is front page of the Lifestyle Section. I bet it's Matt again; he has a talent for hooking up with women who are newsworthy.'

Lu's blood ran cold as she realised that *she* was the person dressed in a Rays shirt, and it hit freezing when she read the words of the headline that swam in front of her face: *Is it love?*

Lu forced herself to focus on the picture of her and

Will that took up the entire top half of the page. His thumb was on her chin and his eyes were blazing with attraction and passion and...love? It really looked like love.

Lu's heart wanted to thump out of her chest.

'Hey, what are you looking at?' Will demanded, and twisted to see what had captured her attention.

She felt his body tense.

'You have got to be freakin' kidding me!'

Lu looked at Will who, she could see, was enraged. He'd made the headlines again—and for all the wrong reasons. Woman-related, not rugby-related.

So the journos were commenting on their relationship? OK, take a breath. It couldn't be that bad, could it?

Lu snatched the paper from his hand and read snippets from the article as she paced the area in front of him. "*Lu Sheppard has been employed by the Stingrays as the official photographer for the last four months... An inside source is quoted as saying that the couple seem very happy together.*"

Will stood up, slapped his hands on his hips and muttered a string of luminous blue swear words. 'What else does it say?' he demanded, his lips compressed in a thin line.

Lu glanced down at the paper again and her voice was tight when she answered him. 'They've never seen you look at anyone like that...have you fallen in love... who am I...?'

Will walked around to the other side of the counter, gripped it with white hands and stared at the floor. 'Hell.'

'There's more.' Lu's hands trembled. '"*Sheppard was absolutely unknown in photography circles before she was appointed as official photographer— introduced, I am told, to the publicity and PR department by Will himself. Was this a little nepotism on Scott's part? However it happened, hanging off Will's coat tails has been a very smart move by Sheppard...her career has been boosted by her association with the Rays and Will Scott. Bravo, Ms Sheppard. Though it can't be the world's toughest job being the sexy head coach's main squeeze.*"'

Lu heard a freight train roaring through her head. 'I thought I was establishing myself, showing people who and what I can do, but it meant nothing. Everybody will now think that I only got the job because of you...'

Will made a move towards her but she held up her hand to ward him off. 'Please don't.'

Will jammed his hands in the pockets of his jeans. 'Lu, it's one opinion—and, crappy as it sounds, it doesn't actually matter. '

'It doesn't matter to *you*! You've established your career. You are respected for what *you've* done, what *you've* achieved. Every job I get from now on people will wonder whether I'm good or just good at sleeping with *you*!'

'You're overreacting, Lu.'

'Don't you dare say that to me!' Lu shouted, fury staining each word. 'You try working your ass off to build something special and then finding out that you're only in the position because you're someone's roll in the hay!'

'You are not just a roll in the hay!' Will protested.

'Funny—that's what I thought I was. Isn't that what

you said I was? Or does a no-strings affair just sound classier?'

'You're upset and you're overreacting.'

Lu bent over, picked up the newspaper and scowled. 'This continues on page two.' Lu turned the page. 'Let's see what else she has to say. *"Aside from Will's love-life, we are all interested to see where he is headed career-wise. My sources tell me that yesterday's match was his last as caretaker coach, that John Carter will be back at the helm on Monday. Will has been headhunted by an Auckland franchise and, as it's the team where he started his professional career, it is expected that he will take their offer of consultant coach. We understand that Will has booked a flight to Auckland tomorrow night."'* Lu closed her eyes against the pain before her head whipped up and her eyes nailed him to the spot. 'You're going home? And you didn't think this was worth mentioning to me?'

'I was going to tell you. Today. I just...'

'You've known about this for a while, haven't you?'

'Yeah. But—'

Her heart cracked. 'You didn't tell me, Will. You didn't tell me about the job offers or that the coach was coming back or that you were going home.' Tears rolled down her cheeks. 'This is what I meant when I said that you don't talk to me!'

'I haven't seen you. I've been away—'

'Don't!' Lu's words whipped around the room. 'Don't make excuses. I've been at the end of my mobile every minute since our last fight. You could've called—told me this. You owed me that.'

Will rubbed his jaw. 'You're right. I just didn't know what to say.'

'*I'm going home on Monday*—that would've been a good start.' Lu scrunched the paper in her hand. 'Don't you think I've had enough surprises in my life? How can you feel so little for me, even if we are just friends, to do this to me? To brush me aside like this? I never expected love from you, Will, but I did expect some measure of respect!'

'I *do* respect you!'

'The hell you do.' Lu wiped her eyes with her free hand. 'You know what? Maybe it *is* just better if you stick to one night stands and walk away. I thought you had changed, but you're still the same selfish, arrogant guy that you were when you were twenty-four. You haven't grown up at all!' Lu slapped the newspaper against his chest. 'I'm done. Thanks for the fun, but we're over. I'm not prepared to bask in your reflected glory, for your popularity and fame to be credited for my hard work. It's too high a price to pay for hot sex and some laughs. And as for not talking to me—take your shriveled-up heart and your issues of control and shove them so far up your backside that they hit your tonsils!'

With those scorching words blistering the room, Lu walked out of his life.

Will sat on the edge of his bed in his Auckland house and looked around the exquisitely decorated room. He absentmindedly played with the cowry shell Lu had given him on the beach which he was now never without.

It looked like a hotel room, he thought. Not a place where someone lived. Where were the photographs?

Lu's messy dressing table? The rows of hooks that held her beads and bangles? It smelled sterile and unused, cold and hard. Of dust and loneliness.

Will looked at the contract lying on the bed and picked it up, not needing to read it again to understand the terms. He hadn't accepted anything, he was still considering all his options, and... Yes, what he was going to do about Lu was a huge part of that. The offer was pretty much the same offer as Kelby had given him—a consultant coach position until an opening for head coach came up.

He didn't want to play second string. He wanted to be in charge. Second string would mean giving up control, working under someone else's vision, under his rules. Not his style. But with the Rays it would only be for six months...Carter would retire at the end of the year.

And, most importantly, Durban held Lu, whom he now realised held his heart. When she'd woken up in his bed six weeks ago he hadn't realised that while he'd been rescuing her she'd been about to save him as well.

Save him from a life of bed-hopping and vacuous women, of brief encounters where bodies touched but souls didn't. From a life devoid of crazy outings—he *would* get her to skydive one day!—and arguments and tender moments and love-fuelled sex.

Her comment about him not changing at all had stung like a scorpion, and while he knew that he *had* changed, maybe he hadn't changed enough. Lu just made him want to be better. He wanted a life with his best friend. He wanted to dance with her on the veranda. He wanted to taste-test her baking and make her laugh. He wanted to be everything she needed, wanted her to be proud of him.

She made him believe in love, in hope, in fairytales.

He was absolutely, comprehensively in love with her. His heart and soul and body were lying at her feet.

The spark, he now realised, had to be nurtured in a fire, and the fire had to be fed. With quiet talks and shared experiences, with the giving and receiving of support.

With communication—which he was seriously crap at.

But Lu—if he could ever talk her around—stubborn, brave and loyal, wouldn't allow the spark to die either; they were both fighters and if they could get past this they could not only keep the fire burning but they could also set the world on fire.

Will stood up and tossed the contract on the bed, reached for the small bag he'd yet to unpack. He was going back to Durban. He'd track Lu down and sort this train wreck of a relationship out. He knew it wouldn't be easy, but he'd give it everything he had.

She would be his.

Fuelled with hope and determination, he dialled for a cab to take him back to the airport. He was going home.

She was going to die. It was official.

Lu sat in the open door of the Cessna, facing out, and her feet dangled into open air. She reached out and gripped the knee of her partner in craziness and thought that along with getting involved with Will this was the stupidest she'd ever done and, she promised herself, would ever do.

Skydiving had been the last thing on her mind when she'd belted out of Durban. She'd originally planned to spend a couple of nights away, but she'd been so entranced with the quiet and the lack of contact with people in Himeville that it had been nearly two weeks before she drove out of the gates of the B&B and a hundred metres down the road saw a sign advertising tandem skydives.

What the hell? she had thought. What could be worse than having your heart shattered into a million pieces?

It was worse—or at the very least just as bad. Oh, dear God, was that a bird a million miles below them?

She didn't want to die... She wanted to go home and crawl into Will's arms and stay there for ever. She wanted to be woken up with his hard body pressed up against her, to hear his deep laugh, to be loved because she was comprehensively, staggeringly, mind-blowingly, fathoms-deep in love with him.

She'd only fully accepted it as she'd walked away from him, and every step that had increased the distance between them had been an effort to accomplish. It had been as if her body recognised him as being the only one and had been fighting to keep her in place.

But, as hard as leaving him had been, she knew that she couldn't have stayed. He didn't value her as much as she valued him, and sadly she couldn't make him. There was nothing left of their relationship. He was gone, and she was sitting in an aeroplane trying to prove a point to herself.

She could do anything she wanted to: she could try new things, meet new people, fall in love. She could friggin' skydive if she set her mind to it.

She had survived her parents' deaths, raising two boys, was establishing a career. She could and *would* survive losing Will.

It would hurt for a while, but then it would fade. Pain, in whatever form it took, always did...she just had to get through it.

She gritted her teeth. *Put one foot in front of the other and keep on truckin'.* She could try pottery lessons again, keep practising her surfing or learn to paint. There were a million things she could try to pass the time while she got used to not having Will in her life, her heart, her mind.

OK, lesson learnt, Lu thought. *Good talk to yourself.*

So, really, did she *actually* have to jump out of this plane now? She was hovering near space, she was scared out of her bracket, but since she'd got this far she knew she could do it if she absolutely had to— she could do *anything* if she absolutely had to—so she didn't really *have* to jump out of the plane, did she?

She could just calmly tell the jump master that she'd changed her mind. She was allowed to do that.

Lu made a slashing movement across her neck, but realised that he hadn't got her message when she and the plane parted company and they went tumbling through unsubstantial nothingness.

Oh, God, this was it...she was going to *diiiiieeeee!*

TWELVE

——

Later that afternoon, Lu rolled her head on her neck, trying to work out the kinks as she parked her car in her garage. Her time in Himeville had turned out to be the break she'd needed to think her life through: cold days, freezing nights, a dead mobile battery and no internet connection. Except for a brief text to the twins as she left Durban, to explain that she was away for a couple of days, she hadn't spoken to anybody for ages.

She had needed not to speak to anyone for that long—needed to take the time to sort out her head and her life—and she was glad that she had. She felt settled, in control, calmer.

After greeting her dogs, who'd been fed by neighbours while she was away, Lu grabbed her bag and headed into her home. In the kitchen she swiped a clean dishcloth over her hair to soak up the raindrops and then wiped the freezing drops from her face.

She wanted a cup of tea, a hot bath and to climb into her huge bed. Himeville suddenly seemed a very long way away, so she deliberately recalled the conclusions she'd come to.

Lu held the back of a kitchen chair and looked out at the wild garden beyond the kitchen. There was no changing the past. It was what it was. Her parents had been irresponsible with money, but it would have been a million times worse if they'd died and left them with nothing... She wouldn't have been able to keep the twins and they would have had to go into the state system.

The thought of it made her shudder.

Her parents had sadly and tragically died, but they'd left them well provided for. She couldn't and wouldn't think about their financial situation before they'd passed...considering *what ifs* and *maybes* just did her head in. If they had lived they would have made a plan, and she knew that no matter what had happened their family would have remained together. They might have been irresponsible and flighty, but their loyalty to each other and their children had been absolute and unwavering.

Wasn't that what had driven her to keep the boys with her? Loyalty? Her parents, she finally realised, would be so proud of her for doing what she had, so maybe it was time to accept that. She hadn't done all the things that normal young adults did, but she could hold her head up high and say that she'd done what she needed to do.

Who cared if one bitchy reporter thought she'd used Will to boost her career? *She* knew she hadn't, Will knew she hadn't, and her bosses knew she hadn't. She had a career she loved and she was damned if she was giving it up!

As for Will... Well, there wasn't much she could do about him. He was back in Auckland and she was alone. She'd spent many long hours wondering what she'd do if he came back, if he offered her a long-distance relationship, if he wanted to resume their friends-with-benefits status. She wouldn't accept either, she'd decided. He had to step up or step away. Friends with benefits just wasn't her style. It was all or nothing. She deserved to have a real and solid connection with a man she knew would stand with her in rain and sunshine, and if he couldn't commit then that was his problem.

'The kettle's boiling dry.'

Lu looked around and blinked at Will, who was standing in the doorway to the hall. She gaped at him for a moment before snapping her mouth closed and sending him an uncertain look. 'Hi. I didn't hear you knock. Sorry.'

Will took two strides across the floor and lifted the kettle from the ring, shut off the gas. 'I didn't knock. I still have my key.'

Lu lifted her eyebrows at his terse tone. He was clearly annoyed, but she couldn't help but admire his broad shoulders in a bottle green sweater. His jeans were worn and faded, frayed at the bottoms where they touched the brown leather of his flat boots. His hair glistened with rain and his jaw was rough with evening stubble. He'd never looked more attractive.

Will found two glass tumblers and slammed them onto the counter. Another loud search produced a bottle of whisky that she hadn't even known was there. He poured a hefty measure in a glass, downed it in one quick swallow and then poured two fingers into both glasses.

'You've driven me to drink,' he muttered.

Taking the glass he held out, Lu looked at it and then looked over at Will, who leant against the kitchen counter, legs crossed in front of him, the light of battle in his eyes. He was more than annoyed—he was mad as hell. And she didn't need to be a rocket scientist to see that all his anger was directed at her.

In an effort to seem unperturbed Lu sat on the dining table and lifted her feet onto the seat of a chair. Will narrowed his eyes at her and she felt the full intensity of his laser stare. OK, this wasn't good. He was past mad and on his way to furious.

'Where the hell have you been?' he demanded through gritted teeth.

Lu ignored her drink and rested her forearms on her thighs. 'In Himeville.'

'I don't even know where that is! You disappear for two weeks and that's all I get? *In Himeville?*'

Lu cocked her head at his temper. She considered saying that the last time she'd checked she was a grown woman and she didn't have to explain to anybody where she was going or why. Something told her that would be placing a lighted match to a powder keg.

'Yes. In Himeville.'

'And you didn't think that I might wonder where you were?'

'I told Kelby that I'd be away for a couple of days,' Lu protested.

'I am not Kelby, and "a couple of days" is two or three—not ten!' Will snapped.

Lu's eyes widened, but Will wasn't finished yet.

'I didn't know where you were—whether you were OK—whether you'd had an accident. The twins didn't know where you were, and neither did your friends!'

'You weren't even here! You were in New Zealand!'

'I was in New Zealand for *ten hours*! If you'd given me a chance to explain I would've told you that it was a flying visit, a turnaround trip.'

'If you had called me and explained then I would've known that!' Lu ripped back.

'I tried to! Every hour for ten sodding days!'

'I needed some time away—to think,' Lu added, her tone hot with aggravation.

Will's roar escalated by thirty decibels. 'I've been going nuts worrying about you! I started calling hospitals, for God's sake.'

'Will you stop shouting at me? I think you're having a bit of an overreaction, here, Will.'

'Overreaction, my ass! Do you know where I should be right now? With my team, helping Carter prepare for a match in three hours, but instead I've been driving past your house praying that you would come home!' Will rubbed his hands down his face. 'You just don't get it, do you?'

Lu lifted her hands in confusion. 'Get what?'

Will stared at a point beyond her shoulder. His eyes were ringed with black, his face was drawn and his hair dishevelled. She saw him haul in a breath and open his mouth to speak, but the words didn't come out.

'Will, I'm sorry you were worried. Given our last

conversation, I thought that you'd left town and that you would be grateful that I was out of your life. I'm fine and—'

'You *still* don't get it.' Will's voice was quiet now. It confused Lu more. 'Well, I'll just have to show you. Give me one minute.'

She watched, open-mouthed, as he whipped his slim mobile phone from his pocket and pushed some buttons. 'Mak—she's back.' He waited a few seconds before speaking again. 'Apparently she's been in Himeville—wherever that is.'

'I'm fine, Mak!' Lu protested, but Will sent her a look that suggested that she shut up.

His eyes never left hers.

He snapped his mobile closed, tossed it onto the counter. Lu echoed his movements and slid off the table, fisted her hands on her hips. 'I've said that I am sorry, but this really has nothing to do with you, and I—'

'Nothing to do with me?'

Lu was still trying to articulate her response when Will grabbed her, pulled her towards him and slanted his lips over hers, his mouth capturing the words she was still trying to say. Before she could think about objecting his tongue slid into her mouth and she lost the ability to think. Blood drained from her head and it was all she could do to keep on her feet as he kissed every objection away. His broad hands snaked up under her clothes and in one deft movement he unsnapped her bra. His warm hands were on her breasts, kneading her nipples to a pulsing ache that hovered just below pain.

Lu whimpered in his mouth, hooked her hands around his neck and boosted herself up. Her legs were anchored around his waist and the juncture of her thighs was riding his erection.

Will held her easily and just kissed her. And then he kissed her some more, open-mouthed and open-hearted. She could feel him vibrating, knew it was from emotion, and pushed her body into his, wanting to absorb every real emotion she could feel emanating from him.

Will sat her on the kitchen counter and held her face, his eyes tracing her features.

Lu bit her lip. 'Will? Why have you stopped?'

His fingers brushed her mouth, her cheek, caressed her ear.

'I needed to know that you were safe—physically, emotionally, mentally.'

Lu's concentration bounced between his words and his actions, her mind and heart trying to decode his words while her libido demanded that he kiss her some more.

She couldn't think.

'How do you think it felt to know that you were hurting and that there was nothing I could do to help you? That I wasn't there to get you out of your far too critical head? That I wasn't there to dry your tears?'

Lu bit her lip, unable to drop her eyes from his.

'There were lots of tears, weren't there, Mermaid?'

The mobile tucked into his back pocket beeped and Will yanked it out with his right hand. 'Kelby and Carter want to know where I am.'

Lu frowned as she jumped off the counter. 'I thought your contract with the Rays was over?'

'That's one of the many things I need to talk to you about. I can't now...' He glanced at his watch. 'I have to get to the stadium. I am late as it is.'

'I agree that we need to talk,' Lu said, her hands twisting his shirt. 'But I'm not sure if you're going to like what I have to say.'

Will placed his hands under her elbows and easily lifted her so that he could look straight into her eyes. The muscles of his arms bunched as they held her up. His expression was pure determination and stubbornness. 'Well, then, you should know this before you say whatever you have to say. No matter where you run, I will find you. I am not letting you out of my life—ever. You are my world—all of my world. You are what I need. You are who I live for. Being with you is all I want.'

Lu felt the cords of tension around her heart snap. She was so stunned that she couldn't even smile. 'I—'

He lowered her to her feet. 'I've got to go, Lu, but take the next couple of hours to get used to the idea that you and I are *it*. That I love you and that neither of us is going anywhere.'

'But—'

Will dropped a kiss on her hair and his hand rubbed her shoulder. He looked worried and rueful, stressed and a little scared. Lu's heart swelled.

'Later—please? I'll be back after the game...around eleven. Wait up for me, OK?'

'Uh...OK.'

It was only long after she heard the front door close

that the weight of his words truly sank in. Will loved her and wanted to be with her. She was going to have her own happily-ever-after.

Lu allowed the bubble of laughter she'd been holding in escape and twirled around, grinning like a loon.

Wait until he came home? She didn't think so.

The fact that the Rays had won and booked their place in the quarter-finals had nothing to do with him and everything to do with his team, Will decided ruefully as he waited to be called to do a post-match televised interview. He'd been less than useless for the entire eighty minutes. He normally had an impressive concentration span, but tonight he'd been ambushed by thoughts of Lu that he couldn't control.

Will looked out over the field, filled with fans of all ages celebrating their win, and wondered if Lu had watched the match. He was happy at the win—of course he was—but his thoughts were just filled with Lu. He'd messed up earlier by yelling at her and then confusing the situation further with that hot kiss. Then he'd added confusion to an already complicated situation by telling her that he was in love with her. Well, he was—but he could've found a more romantic way to tell her.

She was the sum total of what he wanted, needed and wished for.

But what if he wasn't what *she* wanted and needed? What had she meant when she'd stated that he might not like what she had to say? What could that mean? Why hadn't he just taken some more time and talked it through with her? At least he wouldn't be in this agony now.

Will looked at his watch. He'd have to be nice to the sponsors, congratulate his team, and then he could head home. *Damn*, this interviewer was dragging his feet. He shouldn't even be doing this interview, but Carter hated dealing with the press and had handed the responsibility over to him. He suspected that was what would happen for the next six months. Carter would get the glory and he'd do the work. He could live with that. In six months' time the team would be his again.

He wanted to get to Lu, but he also wanted to delay any bad news as long as he could—he wanted to nurture the hope that they had a future. He'd been conscious of the fact that if she said that she didn't want him then he needed to be able to slink off and lick his wounds on his own. He doubted that he could have done any interviews if she'd given him the boot.

He saw the signal to step up and stand in front of the interviewer and hauled in a deep breath. *Be brief, be succinct, get it done and get to Lu.*

Lu, dressed in jeans, a bulky sweater and a cap pulled low over her eyes, watched as Will walked away from the cameras, ducked around a group of kids tackling each other and headed for the players' tunnel. He yanked down his tie and snapped open his collar button, ran his hand through his hair.

He shoved his suit jacket back to push his hands into his pants pockets. He looked tired and worried and near the limit of his patience. A teenage boy ran up to him and his smile wasn't as easy as it normally was as he dashed his signature across a rugby ball. She could see the tension in his shoulders, in the looks he frequently sent towards the exit.

Tucking her iPad under her arm, she jammed her hands into the pockets of her jacket and started to walk over to him.

'Will!' she called, and his head whipped around.

His eyes connected with hers and he angled his head, waiting at the edge of the field for her to reach him. When she was close enough to touch Will held out his hand to her and she saw some of his tension dissipate when her hand slid into his.

'You're here. Why?'

'I have something to show you. Will you come with me?'

'Sure. Where to?'

Lu nodded to the first row of seats in the almost empty stadium. 'Let's sit.'

Will looked around, unconvinced. 'It's rather chilly, and it's going to rain again. Don't you want to go inside?'

Lu shook her head as she led Will up the stairs and sat him down in one of the hard plastic chairs. She crossed her legs and sucked in her breath, looked at the field.

'When we fought I said that you haven't changed, that you are exactly the same as you were when you were twenty-four,' Lu said, her voice jerky. 'That was ugly and cruel and I'm sorry I said it.'

'Sometimes I wonder if it isn't the truth,' Will replied, putting his feet up on the chair in front of him.

'You know it's not, Will. I have the greatest respect for how you turned your life around and I'm so proud of you for doing it. I'm sorry that you still carry such guilt about that period in your life, but maybe you should forgive the young, stupid, dumb jock that you were.'

Lu pulled her iPad out from under her arm and turned it on.

'What's going on, Lu?'

Lu tapped the screen. 'You once asked me if photography was my passion...'

'It is—of course it is,' Will replied, his voice full of conviction as a series of her images flashed across the screen.

Will pointed at the screen as a photo appeared. 'Is this the image for the calendar shoot?'

Lu looked down at the photograph of the naked squad—boy bits hidden—and smiled. They were all laughing, all looking hot, all looking as if they were having the best time of their lives.

'Being in black and white, the image is stark—so why do I want to think it's in colour?' Will tipped his head, thinking. 'It's the emotion, the happiness... it gives an impression of colour.' Will looked at her, utterly amazed. 'It's a fantastic image...they look so happy. How did you do that, Lu? Suggest colour with emotion?'

'Tequila,' Lu quipped. 'Anyway, the reason I'm showing you these is because I've realised that while I adore my job, *you* are my biggest passion.'

More photographs followed, starting with the first one she'd taken of him, looking serious but capable.

'That night I thought I recognised your soul but now—' various shots of Will coaching followed '—I know I do.'

Lu sneaked a look at Will, who seemed to be fascinated at the images of him on the screen.

'Do you know that at least half of the thousands of images I've taken over the last month have been of you?' Lu asked him. 'I love this one,' she said, deliberately chatty, leaning back into his shoulder. Will was crouching on the field, surrounded by his squad, his expression serious but his eyes sparkling. 'It captures how you feel about rugby. *Your* passion.'

'Until you,' Will croaked.

Lu swallowed and blinked away her tears as she gestured to the screen again. 'The following photos capture what I love most about you...'

Will on her veranda eating cake, tossing a rugby ball to Deon on the beach, sharing a joke with Kelby, lying next to the pool in swim-trunks, sunlight glinting off his muscled frame.

Will laughed at some of the images.

Lu snuck her hand into his and tangled her fingers with his. 'This is what I do—what I am, Will. And it seems like you are my favourite subject.' Lu half turned in her seat to face him. 'Before you say anything I need to tell you that I took those huge canvases down from the hall and the living room and put them in the study.'

Will leaned forward and the emotion in his eyes made her blink.

'Why did you take them down, hon? You love those photographs.'

Lu pursed her lips. 'I do, but it's time to move on. I have so many photos of my parents and the twins scattered around. I don't want them to dominate my house and my thoughts any more. I want photos of us and you—family and new memories.'

Will's eyes smoked over. 'Lu...God...'

'My parents are gone, and I miss them, but it's time to let them go. The twins are leading their own lives and making their own decisions and I need to move on.'

'Move on to what, Lu?'

Lu smiled gently. 'You, me, *us.*'

Will's voice sounded uncharacteristically emotional when he finally answered. 'So there is an us?'

Lu stared at him, completely nonplussed. Judging by his the-axe-is-about-to-fall expression, Will still had doubts about her—doubts that she loved him. How could that be?

'Why wouldn't there be?'

'Because you said you had something to tell me that I wouldn't like...'

Lu had to smile. How could her smart man have got this so wrong?

'I was going to tell you that I want more from you than just being friends with benefits! You still look doubtful...*why?*'

'I just can't believe how lucky I am.' Will rubbed the back of his neck, his eyes filled with emotion. 'I just wish you could see yourself through my eyes—wish you could understand how extraordinary I think you are. You are a brilliant photographer and an amazingly unselfish, giving person. And I'm driven and ambitious and frequently selfish. I'm tough, and I'm scared that I will hurt you.'

'Will you cheat on me?' Lu asked, cocking her head.

'No.'

Will's answer was rock-fast and true. Lu hadn't even needed to ask the question. She'd already known the answer in her heart. But she'd thought that he needed to say it.

'Will you demand that I stop work?'

Denial, hot and fast, flashed in his eyes. 'No. You love your job—why would I do that?'

Lu looked down at their linked hands. 'Will, don't put me on a pedestal, because I *will* fall off. I did one good thing, and I'm proud I did it, but it's not all of who I am. I can be bitchy and moody, and I will have days when I want to bury myself in my studio and not come out. There will be days of tears and frustration, moments of madness, hours of irrationality. I will be occasionally insecure and will probably make some huge mistakes. So will you. But, to paraphrase that great blonde, Marilyn Monroe, if we can't handle each other at our worst then we don't deserve each other at our best. I'm not an angel, and neither are you, and I'd hate it if we were. I'm standing here, trying to tell you that I am just Lu...'

'And I think you are perfect—flaws and all.'

'And that I love you.' Lu's eyes filled with emotion.

Satisfaction flickered across his face as he rose to his feet. 'And I am *so* in love with you.'

Will lifted his hands to cradle her face, his eyes blazing with love for her. Lu sank into his kiss and joy bubbled up inside her as she leaned into his embrace, felt those strong arms envelop her.

She was where she belonged...finally. This man was her home.

She recognised a sound—the click and whirr of a camera going off...after all, along with Will's laughter it was her favourite sound in the world. Lu lifted her mouth from Will's and turned to see a dark-haired woman standing just below them.

'I'm Lin Reynolds. Can I ask you a couple of questions?' she demanded, looking up and into their faces.

Will's eyes blazed with fury. 'No. And isn't it a bit late for you to be asking questions? I thought you wrote articles first and checked your facts later.'

Lin Reynolds...the author of the article that had sent her running. Lu lifted her eyebrows as the woman tossed her head and scoffed at Will's statement.

'Like you would've answered any questions about *that* photograph!'

'Probably not.' Will wrapped his hand around the back of Lu's neck and his eyes softened as he looked at her. Happiness, satisfaction and relief blazed from his eyes.

'Go away,' he said, without taking his eyes off her face.

'What do you see in her, anyway?' the pushy reporter demanded.

Good grief, this woman was a pain in the ass.

Lu tipped up her head and sent him a naughty grin. 'Yeah, Will, what *do* you see in me, *anyway*?'

He looked straight into her eyes and he smiled softly. 'I think she's brave, loyal and loving. Sexy as hell, too.'

'Just because she was a glorified nanny?'

That was what she had thought—but she hadn't been. She had been the twins' link to their parents, their port in every storm, a solid and consistent loving presence in their lives.

She'd be the same for Will too.

And they'd share some very hot sex. *Whoo!*

'I know that look,' Will whispered, and grinned.

'You should,' Lu murmured, her eyes sliding to the right. 'She's still here...'

'She's persistent. I'll give her that,' Will said, and on a frustrated sigh he turned back to the irritating journalist. 'Having fun, butting in on a very private moment? And, by the way, what were *you* doing at nineteen? Sex, drugs and rock and roll? You just threw a very big rock through a very big glass house, Ms Reynolds.'

The woman folded her arms across her chest. 'I still think there's a lot more to this story than you are telling...just like there is a lot more to your divorce than you want everyone to know.'

'My divorce is now very old, very tedious news. The only thing you need to know is that I love Lu and—'

'I love him,' Lu chipped in, her grin widening at the thought.

'And...?' Lin leaned forward eagerly. 'Are you getting married? Making it legal?'

'We're not going to tell you that,' Will retorted.

'But...what else can I tell my readers?'

Lu, as she snuggled into Will's side, felt sorry for this sad woman who lived her life reporting on other people's lives. 'Really, Ms Reynolds, there isn't a story here. Will and I are together, we're crazy about each other, and we're going to be deliciously, boringly, brain-meltingly happy. Loyal, loving...monogamous. No fuss, no drama. He's going to keep coaching. I'm going to keep clicking.'

Will looked at her approvingly. 'That is it in a nut-shell.' He looked at Lin and grinned. 'You can quote us on that.'

When the reporter was out of earshot Will wrapped his other arm around her waist and yanked her into him. 'Boringly, brain-meltingly happy, Mermaid?'

Lu grinned. 'It just tumbled out.'

'It sounds good to me. Let's go home.'

'Yours or mine?'

Will brushed his thumb across her lips. 'I'm really hoping that yours can become mine, too. At least for the next five years, since I've signed a contract with the Rays which will keep me here that long. I don't want to spend another night without you. You OK with that?'

'Very. I just want you...for always.'

Will's lips touched her in a love-soaked kiss that saturated every atom of her body, promising love and devotion and protection. Lu sighed into his mouth as she reached out and grabbed the shiny, star-spangled feeling of happiness.

She was, finally, Lu. And best of all she was monstrously in love with a man who loved her back. Life, she thought, as they walked with their arms around each other towards the exit, didn't get much more breathtakingly splendid than this.

EPILOGUE

——

Seven months later, on Lu's thirtieth birthday, her three men stood in front of the guests gathered on her big veranda to celebrate her birthday. Her breath caught in her throat. The twins were only just shy of Will's height—her two blond, brave, *nice* boys.

And Will, looking so very hot in black pants and a white cotton shirt that showed off his gorgeous body to perfection, stood between them, his hands jammed into his pockets, totally relaxed. Like Nate and Dan, he also wanted to make a speech, but unlike her brothers he didn't need key cards to remind him of what he wanted to say.

Will had a very clever mouth—in the bedroom and out.

Nate cleared his throat as Daniel tapped a spoon against the stem of his glass. The room quietened and Lu caught Will's eye and smiled at his wink.

'Thank you all for joining Daniel, Will and I at this occasion to celebrate Lu's thirtieth birthday. As most of you know, Lu raised us after our parents died when we were eight, and about a year ago we left her on her own to go off to university. We were terrified that she was going to hide out in this house and start talking to her cats.'

Laughter rumbled as Daniel took over the speech. 'Instead she met Will, and we're pretty chuffed because she chose someone who can organise tickets to any rugby game we want and who can invite us to practise with the Rays. Other than that, he's pretty useless.'

Will rolled his eyes as the boys slapped him on the shoulder. *Yeah, useless,* Lu thought. Except when they over-exceeded their allowance and tapped Will for a loan. Or when they needed advice on girls, or their studies, or just to chat. Will had slid into his role of advisor and older brother and the twins valued his presence in their lives. He was now so much more to them than Lu's live-in lover, and it made her heart jump into her throat just thinking about the bond they shared. If anything ever happened to her she knew they would never lose Will.

Daniel continued. 'But he does make Lu happy, and we cannot thank him enough for that.'

Tears brimmed in Lu's eyes and she saw Will's Adam's apple bob up and down as he swallowed his own emotion.

'So, Lu, we bought you another skydiving jump—not that you really did it the first time.'

Lu borrowed one of Will's favourite expressions. 'Hell, no!' she called out.

She'd told them that she'd skydived in Himeville but none of them had believed her, insisting that she was making it up to get out of really doing it. Lu insisted that she didn't care if they believed her or not, but the argument raged on.

'You are such a *girl*!' Nate said in mock disgust.

'And proud of it,' Lu retorted as the whole room laughed.

'Anyway,' Daniel continued, 'your real gift is a sort of combination gift...from Will, Nate and I.'

Lu tipped her head, curious.

Nate held her eyes. 'We'd like to give you the house, Lu. *This* house. We'd like to sign our shares in it over to you. Partly to say thank you for providing us with a safe place to be when our lives fell apart. Thank you for being so brave and loving us so much to do that.'

'And we'd really like you to live here with Will, but if he ever moves you to Auckland and coaches their team we will *not* be happy!' Nate added.

'Neither will I!' Kelby shouted from the back of the room.

Lu held her hand to her throat as tears streamed down her face. Will was a blurry mass of muscle as he stepped forward and took her hand. Lu blinked and he came into focus, a glinting ring between his thumb and forefinger.

Lu gaped at the aquamarine and diamond ring and then at him. 'Wha—?'

Will shook his head to silence her. 'My part of the gift is this, but unfortunately for you, it comes with me. I'd like to live here with you in this house, as your husband, your lover, your best friend. Marry me, Lu?'

'You want to get married again?' Lu managed to stutter.

'Not again...for the first time. Properly. Because I am utterly in love with you. Say yes, Lu.'

'I love you too. Yes. Of course!'

Will slipped the ring onto her finger as the room erupted into cheers.

'Say yes to skydiving, baby,' Will said as he bent to kiss her.

'Anything you want...' Lu replied, swept away by the emotional moment as she reached up to meet his mouth. Then her eyes narrowed and she slapped a hand on his chest. 'What? What did you just ask me? You sneaky skunk!'

Will just laughed, slid his arms around her and kissed her.

Lu sighed and sank into his embrace. She would argue with him about skydiving later...

Again.

* * * * *

COMING NEXT MONTH FROM

 HARLEQUIN®

KISS™

Available December 17, 2013

#45 THE DANCE OFF
Ally Blake

Dancing lessons...? Ryder Fitzgerald can't think of anything worse! But as electricity crackles in the studio between him and dance coach Nadia Kent, restricting their chemistry to the dance floor becomes a challenge.... Only question is, who'll make the first move?

#46 MR. (NOT QUITE) PERFECT
Jessica Hart

Journalist Allegra Fielding has to find a man willing to take part in a *makeover*—fast! Time to blackmail her roommate, Max.... But Max is going to enjoy proving to Allegra that there's nothing hotter than a man who's a little rough around the edges....

#47 CONFESSIONS OF A BAD BRIDESMAID
Jennifer Rae

Nothing about bridesmaid Olivia Matthews is welcome at this society wedding. The *only* silver lining is best man Edward Winchester. Okay, he's uptight, but he also kisses like an X-rated dream. If only he'd stop being so chivalrous...!

#48 AFTER THE PARTY
Jackie Braun

Chase has been too busy saving his family's business to find much to laugh about recently. He might have agreed to throw a themed party, but that doesn't mean he's off duty just yet! Until he meets party planner Ella. Something about her tempts him to loosen his tie, take off his suit jacket and finally have some fun....

YOU CAN FIND INFORMATION ON UPCOMING HARLEQUIN® TITLES, FREE EXCERPTS AND MORE AT WWW.HARLEQUIN.COM.

HKCNM1213

SPECIAL EXCERPT FROM

 HARLEQUIN®

KISS™

She should *never* have agreed to be
a part of this wedding...

CONFESSIONS OF A
BAD BRIDESMAID

"I thought you were having fun."

He moved closer. She looked cold. He wanted to warm
her up.

"I was. I like to have fun."

She blinked at him and he moved even closer, letting his
shoulder rest against hers. Just in case she fell. Her lips parted
and he almost forgot where he was and, for a moment, *who*
he was.

Her hair was wild around her face and her eyes were glancing
at his lips. His entire body went hard and he couldn't move.
He watched as she licked her full, bouncy lips. This woman was
dangerous. One of those women who made you forget. But he
couldn't forget. He could never forget.

You're being foolish, he reminded himself as he dragged his
eyes away from her plump lips. Kissing someone like Olivia
would not help. Dragging a woman into his life was not something he could do.

He could see her thinking. He was sure she could see him
thinking. Wanting to do something he shouldn't. Wishing it
was him who'd had those glasses of champagne. Maybe then
he wouldn't think so much.

Her blue eyes swivelled back up to him and he saw the question in them. The air was thick and heavy and so was her need. He answered it automatically by pulling her in even closer.

"You feel nice," she murmured as she snuggled in, and let out a little mew.

"Olivia, are you all right?"

"I am now," she murmured, pulling herself closer.

That wasn't what he'd wanted her to do. Being out here with Olivia was a selfish indulgence. This was getting out of hand.

"Olivia, you're too…"

The word *intoxicating* embedded itself into his mind as her scent circled around his face. She *was* intoxicating. She lifted her head and her eyes darkened. He knew the look on her face. Pure desire. He was sure she could see the same look on his face.

"Too what?"

She licked her bottom lip and his mind went blank. All thoughts of guilt disappeared and something more animal took over. All her lipstick had come off. Her lips were bare and delicious. He moved a single finger up to trace them and she stood still. Her breath warmed his finger. With his thumb, he swept a line past her open lips and she responded by poking her pink tongue out. It caught his thumb and he'd never felt anything more erotic.

"Too much," he whispered.

Pick up CONFESSIONS OF A BAD BRIDESMAID by Jennifer Rae, on sale January 2014, wherever Harlequin® books and ebooks are sold.

Copyright © 2013 by Jennifer Birchall

HKEXP1213